Judge Jackie:
Disorder in the Court

Book & Lyrics by
Christopher Dimond

Music by
Michael Kooman

Based on a concept by
Van Kaplan

A SAMUEL FRENCH ACTING EDITION

SAMUEL
FRENCH

FOUNDED 1830

SAMUELFRENCH.COM
SAMUELFRENCH-LONDON.CO.UK

MUSIC USE NOTE

IMPORTANT BILLING AND CREDIT REQUIREMENTS

**Originally produced
By the Pittsburgh CLO, Pittsburgh, PA
Van Kaplan, Executive Director**

CHARACTERS

JACKIE – (40s/50s) Sharp-witted, cynical television judge.

HENRY – (40s) Jackie's mild-mannered, insecure bailiff. Also plays: **JORGE DE AMORE** – A sultry telenovela character from Jackie's childhood.

SHANE – (40s) Smarmy television executive. Also plays: **ALLISTER DICASTRO** – Jackie's pompous ex-husband; **AGENT** – A government Agent. **ZOMBIE** – A Zombie; **BOOMING VOICE** – Of the Great Xantos on High.

ONE MAN & ONE WOMAN (20s – 30s)

Who play:

BROOKS AND MARJORIE – Renaissance Fair performers.

DUANE AND LUANNE – Red-neck Doomsday preppers.

TREAT AND POO-BEAR – Privileged wannabe gangstas.

BRITLEY SPANX – An obnoxious teen pop star.

FRANK SPANX – Her indulgent father.

YOUNG ALLISTER – A kinder version of Allister.

MAMA – Henry's elderly mother.

DONOR GUY AND DONOR LADY – A bit elderly couple.

CATFISH GUY – A deluded man.

BUILDING LADY – A woman in love with a monument.

KITTY – A furry.

YOUNG JACKIE – Jackie in middle school.

YOUNG JORGE – A younger Jorge De Amore.

SETTING

A television studio in the city of the production.

TIME

The present.

AUTHORS' NOTE

The script includes a number of specific regional references. In this version of the script, they are in [brackets] and **bold**. It is the authors' intent that these sections of dialogue should be altered to give the show a local flavor particular to the specific region of each individual production.

ACT I

*(At rise: As the audience filters in, the actors mingle with them. **HENRY**, dressed in a bailiff's uniform, enters.)*

HENRY. Hello there, ladies and gentlemen. Welcome to the Judge Jackie Justice show. If anyone is here for the taping of *So You Think You Can Twerk*, you're one theatre over. We're going to get started in just a couple of minutes, but before we do, we have a special treat for you tonight. Judge Jackie has graciously agreed to come out for a brief photo opportunity. And, if we're especially lucky, she may even take a few questions. So, ladies and gentlemen, please give a warm welcome to Judge Jackie Justice.

*(**JACKIE** enters.)*

Would anyone like to have their picture taken with the judge? Don't be shy. Come on up, and I can snap a quick photo with your smart phone.

(He lets this play out.)

Unfortunately, the judge has to get back stage to get ready for taping. Let's give her one more round of applause.

*(**JACKIE** exits.)*

I'd like to once again welcome you to our nationwide tour of the number one show on daytime television, *Judge Jackie Justice.*

For those of you who don't know me, which, judging from my fan mail is most of you, my name is Henry Winslow. I will be your humble bailiff and emcee this afternoon. So, good afternoon [**Local City**].

HENRY. *(cont.)* Before we begin, I need to remind you all to take this opportunity to turn off your cell phones. Also, the use of flash photography and other recording devices is strictly prohibited. Judge Jackie can get a bit, well, let's just say that there's a tabloid reporter in **[Nearby City]**who won't be sitting comfortably anytime soon.

Our show this evening does involve the use of bright lights and smoke, so don't be alarmed if you see anything like that. In the unlikely event of an emergency, exits are located at the back of the studio and behind this curtain to my left, and most importantly, in the event of a true emergency, the bar will be open during intermission.

Now, jury duty in Judge Jackie's court doesn't work quite the way you may be used to. Jurors are often asked to serve the court in somewhat unconventional ways. For instance, Judge Jackie likes to begin each case with a burst of enthusiasm, so all jurors are expected to sing the Judge Jackie theme song. For those of you who may need a little brush up, our music director, **[Pianist's Name]**, is here to help. Here's how it goes. Judge Jackie will sing...

[MUSIC NO. 00: "LEARNING JUDGE JACKIE"]

JUDGE JACKIE JUSTICE.

And you will echo her with...

HENRY & ALL.

JUDGE JACKIE JUSTICE.

HENRY.

Shall we try it? Hit it, **[Pianist's Name]**. Five, six, seven, eight.

JUDGE JACKIE JUSTICE.

(**HENRY** *motions for audience to sing, all available cast members sing with the audience from off stage.*)

ALL.

JUDGE JACKIE JUSTICE.

Henry. Oh, come on.

JUDGE JACKIE JUSTICE.

ALL.

JUDGE JACKIE JUSTICE.

HENRY.

JUDGE JACKIE JUSTICE.

ALL.

JUDGE JACKIE JUSTICE.

HENRY.

JUDGE JACKIE JUSTICE.

HENRY & ALL.

JUDGE JACKIE JUSTICE.

(**HENRY** *motions to cut everyone off.*)

HENRY. Excellent.

Alright, ladies and gentlemen, we're ready to get started. Sit back, relax, and get ready to enjoy the number one show on daytime television because we are rolling in five, four, three, two…

[MUSIC NO. 01: "JUDGE JACKIE JUSTICE"]

(**JACKIE**'s *intro video begins on a small screen. We hear music and a voice over. As the voice over continues, the curtain opens, and the video is seen, much larger.*)

VOICE OVER. She's the quick-witted judge whose passion for justice took her from the mean streets of Brooklyn to the highest courts in the land. And now, she's bringing her patented brand of no-nonsense juris prudence

straight into your living room five days a week. She is...
Judge Jackie Justice.

> *(Enter JACKIE.)*

JACKIE.
> TAKE YOUR SEATS AND PAY ATTENTION.
> SHUT YOUR TRAP AND ZIP YOUR LIP.
> COURT'S IN SESSION, NOW THERE'S NO REFUTIN'
> JACKIE'S SHOOTIN' STRAIGHT FROM THE HIP.
>
> THERE'S NO HIGHER COURT THAN MY COURT.
> AT LEAST NOT ON YOUR TV.
> I'M A TRUTH MACHINE, THERE'S NOT DENYING,
> DON'T TRY LYING IN FRONT OF ME.
>
> DON'T YOU GIVE ME NO PHONY BALONEY
> CAUSE FALSE TESTIMONY
> WILL ALWAYS FAIL.
>
> DON'T YOU GIVE ME NO SNARKY MALARKEY
> OR I'LL THROW YOUR ASS
> RIGHT IN JAIL.
>
> HERE THE VERDICTS ALL ARE FINAL.
> SO DON'T STAMMER HEM OR HAW.
> IN MY COURTROOM CASES ARE ALL CIVIL,
>
> DON'T YOU SNIFF AND SNIVEL,
> SAVE YOUR DRIVEL, MY WORD IS LAW.

JACKIE (ECHOED BY ALL).
> JUDGE JACKIE JUSTICE.
> JUDGE JACKIE JUSTICE.
> JUDGE JACKIE JUSTICE.
> JUDGE JACKIE JUSTICE.
> JUDGE JACKIE JUSTICE.

HENRY. What you are about to see is real. Really real. The participants are not actors, they are actual people. They have agreed to come here today to air their very real grievances and abide by the distinctively real decisions of Judge Jackie Justice. Today, we're coming to you from historic **[City, State of production]**, as

Judge Jackie brings her unique judicial stylings to the birthplace of [**List of three things local city is known for, the third of which is weird or silly**].

JACKIE.

SO YOU THINK THAT YOU'RE PRETTY DAMN WITTY,
WELL, HONEY, I PITY
STUPIDITY.

AND MY ONE SIXTY TWO POINT IQ SAYS THAT YOU
HAVE GOT NOTHING ON ME.

I'M THE KING, THE QUEEN, THE SULTAN.
AND LIKE SPRINGSTEEN, I'M THE BOSS.
AND MY RULE HERE IS SO SUPREME THAT YOU WISH
YOU COULD BE THIS SHREWISH.
I'M THE JEWISH DIANA ROSS.

JUDGE JACKIE JUSTICE.
JUDGE JACKIE JUSTICE.
JUDGE JACKIE JUSTICE.
JUDGE JACKIE JUSTICE.
JUDGE JACKIE JUSTICE.

Alright, Henry, let's get this show on the road.

[MUSIC NO. 01A: "FIRST CASE"]

HENRY. This is the plaintiff, Brooks Billingston. He claims that the defendant's negligence caused him severe bodily harm. He is suing for six hundred dollars.

(*Enter* **BROOKS**, *in everyday clothes.*)

This is the defendant, Marjorie Merriweather. She claims that the plaintiff is "too stupid for words".

(*Enter* **MARJORIE**.)

We now call to order The Case of the Renaissance Reenactor's Piping Pizza Pie.

JACKIE. Mr. Billingston, what is the nature of the injury you claim the defendant caused?

(**BROOKS** *and* **MARJORIE** *speak with pronounced local dialects – dialogue can be changed as necessary.*)

BROOKS. She burned the roof a my mouth with the cheese. I's just minding my own bidness –

JACKIE. Whoa, whoa, whoa. What?

BROOKS. I said, this no good nut job burned the roof a my mouth with that there molten mozzarella.

JACKIE. My pet dog Sandra Day O'Corgi speaks more clearly than you, Mr. Billingston, and she drools less, too.

MARJORIE. *Yer* Honor, allow me. I work *dahn* there at Lady Marjorie Merriweather's House of Mutton, which *yer prolly* know is the most historically accurate eatery *dahn* the [**Local Bucolic County**] Renaissance Faire.

JACKIE. And we're out of the frying pan and into the fire.

MARJORIE. I's down there last Tuesday, when in *burst this clahn*!

[MUSIC 01B: "BROOKS AND MARJORIE"]

(A flashback begins, they tear away their clothes, revealing ridiculous Renaissance garb.)

BROOKS. G'den, Lady Marjorie. Be a lass, and fetch us ye oldey slice of pepperoni pizza.

MARJORIE. By the gods of authentic historical re-enactment, this be'th late Sixteenth Century England, if thou want'st thy pizza, I suggest thou hie thyself hence to a time and place whence pizza actually exists!

BROOKS. A-vaunt thou, baggage. I am thy champion of non-contact joust.

MARJORIE. Thou shalt ne'er have thy pizza by this hand.

BROOKS. 'Sblood. Thence upon yon ground, I challengeth thou to a duel.

MARJORIE. Thou durst not.

BROOKS. I durst. Caliban, forsooth!

(He selects an audience member.)

Ah, there thou art, Caliban. This is my mute manservant Caliban. He fighteth all my duels for me.

MARJORIE. Ariel!

(She selects an audience member.)

This is my mute scullery maid, Ariel. She shalt o'er power thy mute manservant Caliban.

BROOKS. Prepare thyself, Caliban.

(They position the audience members to square off.)

MARJORIE. On second thought, pools of blood have not proven good for business at yon House of Mutton, e'er since the great pot pie duel of aught seven. A battle of wits!

BROOKS. A battle of wits!

(Beat, as they look at the audience members.)

Nay.

MARJORIE. Nay.

BROOKS. No battle of wits.

MARJORIE. A staring contest!

BROOKS. A staring contest! If Caliban shouldst win, thou shalt bak'st mine pizza.

MARJORIE. And if Ariel shouldst win, thou shalt leave mine shoppe, whereupon thou shalt proclaim thyself a knave, a fiend, and a wayward whoreson [**Local Insult**]!

BROOKS. On thy mark!

MARJORIE. Get'st thou set!

BROOKS. Go'eth!

*(The audience members stare. **BROOKS** jumps in front of the female audience member.)*

Zounds! Is that ? [**Local Newscaster or B-List Celebrity**]?

(Hopefully, she flinches.)

Ha-ha! The day is't mine.

MARJORIE. And so, yer Honor, by mine honor, I gave the *tool* his pizza.

(She hands him a slice of pizza, he takes a bite.)

BROOKS. Ow. Jethuth. The cheeth. Ith hot. Ith tho hot. I am thlain. The reth…ith…thilenth.

JACKIE. You're joking, right? This whole thing is part of your act, yes?

MARJORIE. Trust me, *yinz* Honor, he ain't that good of an actor –

JACKIE. Ms. Merryweather, if I were interested in the opinions of simpletons, I'd pay attention at Thanksgiving dinner.

BROOKS. Ha. She told yer sorry –

JACKIE. Can it, Tinman, I'm talking now. Am I mistaken, or are you suing this woman because you burned your tongue on pizza cheese?

BROOKS. So?

JACKIE. It's pizza cheese. It might be hot. It's supposed to be hot, you foppish buffoon!

BROOKS. What yinz call me?

JACKIE. Ruling for the defendant. You've been burned, and we're adjourned.

(**HENRY** *ushers them out.*)

HENRY. We're clear, your Honor. Would you like to take five before our next case?

JACKIE. You'd better believe it. I can hear my pastrami on rye calling from here.

[MUSIC NO. 01C: "SHANE'S ENTRANCE"]

(**HENRY** *exits. Enter* **SHANE**.)

SHANE. Ms. Justice? Wait a second… Justice? And you're a judge. Just got that.

JACKIE. Who the hell are you?

SHANE. Shane Shankleman. The new NBS Senior Vice President of Reality Television and Online Videos of Adorable Cats.

JACKIE. I'm on my pre-lunch lunch.

SHANE. Jackie-cakes… Can I call you Jackie-cakes?

JACKIE. No.

SHANE. Jackie-cakes, there's been a bit of a dustup down at the network, and I'm afraid you're at the center of it.

JACKIE. Me?

SHANE. You've seen the latest ratings?

JACKIE. No. I –

SHANE. It seems your little show has suffered a rather sudden drop. In fact, you're now mired somewhere between *Law & Order: Special Tax Fraud Unit* and *How I Slept With a Bunch of Women Before I Met Your Mother*.

JACKIE. That's not possible.

SHANE. Most of the suits at NBS are throwing around big words like cancellization.

JACKIE. You are aware that that's not a word, correct?

SHANE. Nevertheless, they want to cancellize you.

JACKIE. Cancel me? No. They can't.

SHANE. They can. And they can. Because they lack my visionacity. I'm sure I don't have to tell you about the other shows I've visionacinated, what with the success of *The Millionaire Pregnant Teen Widows' Bachelorette Matchmaker*.

JACKIE. Never heard of it.

SHANE. Or *America's Got Diabetes.*

JACKIE. Tell me that's not a real thing.

SHANE. Or my biggest hit, *Kitten Chews on Fork Stuck in Electrical Socket.*

> *(He pulls out an iPhone and shows her a short clip, from which we hear the horrifying soundtrack.)*

JACKIE. Goodness gracious.

SHANE. I know. We're planning a spin-off. This little cat's gonna be a star. Well, a cat that looks a lot like this one.

JACKIE. What's any of this got to do with me?

[MUSIC NO. 02: "REALITY TV"]

SHANE.

> FOLKS THINK REALITY IS SOME KIND OF BORE.
> CAUSE THEIR DAILY LIVES ARE A TOTAL SNORE.
> BUT THANKS TO ME THAT ISN'T TRUE ANYMORE.
> CREATIVE EDITS,
> BIG SPLASHY CREDITS.
>
> NOW YOU'VE GOT SOMETHING THAT THEY'RE DYING TO
>   SEE.
> YOU'VE GOT REALITY T.V.

JACKIE. Are you actually insane enough to tell me how to –

SHANE.

> SPICE UP THE SHOW A BIT AND I GUARANTEE
> YOU'LL HAVE "OOH" AND "AH", YOU'LL HAVE "O.M.G."
> AND THEN THROW IN A DOSE OF CELEBRITY.
> STARS ON THE DOCKET.
> RATINGS SKYROCKET.
>
> RAMP UP THE DRAMA AND I THINK YOU'LL AGREE,
> YOU'VE GOT REALITY T.V.

JACKIE. Get out of my courtroom.

SHANE.

> BUSINESS IS SLOW.
> SUFFICE TO SAY
> YOUR SHOW GETS LESS AND LESS SUCCESSFUL BY THE DAY.
>
> AND EVERY YEAR
> YOUR RATINGS DROP.
> BUT SOMEONE'S HERE WHO KNOWS THE WAY TO MAKE IT
>   STOP.

The end of the day, Jackie-pie. I've got until the end of the day today to turn things around. If we can't boost ratings, your show is as dead as a kitten that chewed on a fork stuck in an electrical socket.

> YOU WANT TO SEE YOUR NUMBERS START TO INFLATE?
> EVERY NOW AND THEN YOU MUST EXAGGERATE.
> WHAT JUICY EVIDENCE CAN YOU FABRICATE?
> THE NETWORK'S HITLESS,
> MAKE UP A WITNESS.

SO, BID FAREWELL TO YOUR INTEGRITY.
ONLY LOSERS CLING TO LEGALITY.
THINGS LIKE MORALITY DON'T MATTER, YOU SEE.
BABY, YOU'LL MAKE IT
IF YOU JUST FAKE IT.
LET'S MAKE REALITY T.V.

It's merely a question of exactly which patented Shane Shankleman ratings-boost technique to employ. Ooh! Are you familiar with *Celebrity Couples Court?*

JACKIE. *Celebrity Couples Court?*

SHANE. Judge Allister something or other.

JACKIE. DiCastro.

SHANE. Hm?

JACKIE. Judge Allister DiCastro.

SHANE. See? Even an aging recluse like you knows who he is.

JACKIE. Oh, I know who he is alright.

SHANE. Number one in your time slot, that's who he is. Across all demographicals. If we make your show more like *CCC*, we're sure to boost ratings. Do you know any celebrities?

JACKIE. No.

SHANE. I met Mr. T at a Burger King once, but I don't know if that's enough to get him on the show. Plus he neglected to put pickles on my Whopper. Has that Honey Boo Boo kid OD'd yet?

JACKIE. Is that a person?

SHANE. I wish she'd OD'd. Or had half the legal troubles of Britley Spanx. Wait a minute! Britley Spanx.

JACKIE. Who?

SHANE. Britley Spanx. Teen pop sensation and the mother of all celebrity controversy magnets. Why, she once got arrested during her own wedding, and then got divorced before she made bail.

JACKIE. Listen to me, Shane. This show is about real people. And while real people may be morons, they're my morons. I'll be damned if I'm going to let some braindead celebrities use my show as a platform to peddle their hoochie mama record albums, or their hoochie mama clothing line, or their hoochie mama breakfast cereals. I make a difference in people's lives, just like Jorge de Amor.

[MUSIC #03: ALLISTER DREAM #1]

SHANE. Who's Jorge de Amor?

JACKIE. What?

SHANE. You said you make a difference just like Jorge de Amor.

JACKIE. No I didn't. Why would I say that? That would be ridiculous. The point is, my show matters to real people, unlike that sell-out sideshow *Celebrity Couple's Court.*

SHANE. I'll tell you what I'm going to do: I'll watch this next little case of yours, and determinate exactly what it is that *Celebrity Couple's Court* has that your show doesn't. Yessir, you could learn a lot from Judge Allister DiCastro.

(He exits. **YOUNG ALLISTER** *appears.)*

YOUNG ALLISTER. Did someone say my name?

JACKIE. Allister? What are you doing here?

YOUNG ALLISTER. May I have this dance?

JACKIE. Dance? Oh please, you really think I'm going to – Allister, you look so young.

YOUNG ALLISTER. I may be young, Jackie, I may be a poor law student who could barely get up the nerve to ask you out between Torts and Civil Procedure, but that doesn't mean that swearing to spend the rest of our lives together hasn't made today the best day of my life.

JACKIE. Did we really dance like this?

(They sing.)

YOUNG ALLISTER.
OHH.

JACKIE & YOUNG ALLISTER.
 OHH.

YOUNG ALLISTER. I swear, Jackie, even when you're a Supreme Court Justice and I'm a struggling public defender, I will make sure that you're always as happy as you are right now.

(An older version of **ALLISTER** *appears.)*

ALLISTER. Run along, sport. You don't quite know the steps.

JACKIE. Allister. Now that's the way I remember you.

(He cuts in. **YOUNG ALLISTER** *exits.)*

ALLISTER. You know, of all my ex-wives, you were always my favorite. Well, second favorite. Top three.

JACKIE. I'm not hearing this.

ALLISTER. What you should be hearing is everything that Shane fellow has to say. He's one sharp cookie. And roguishly handsome to boot. Take his advice, Jackie, and someday you'll be as happy as me.

(He disappears.)

JACKIE. I'm the highest paid personality on television, Allister. I've won twenty two Emmy Awards. I was on the New York Supreme Court. I didn't work my way up from nothing to let you –

(Enter **HENRY**.*)*

HENRY. Your Honor?

JACKIE. Henry?

HENRY. You're shouting at no one.

JACKIE. Sometimes I shout at no one, Henry. It's part of my charm.

HENRY. Yes, your Honor.

JACKIE. Henry? Have you ever felt as though there was something in your life that was somehow…missing?

HENRY. No, your Honor. I've never felt as though there were anything missing. From my life. Nothing at all.

JACKIE. No. Neither have I. I was only wondering.

HENRY. Of course, your Honor. How could there possibly be something missing from your life? You've got the number one show on daytime television.

JACKIE. You're right, Henry, a woman with the number one show on daytime television could never feel as though there were something missing from her life, could she?

HENRY. Your Honor?

[MUSIC NO. 04: "I'LL GET IT BACK"]

JACKIE. Henry, I want you to find me the most ridiculous case we've got on the docket. Let's knock this next one out of the park.

HENRY. Right away, your Honor.

(**HENRY** exits.)

JACKIE.

I'VE ALWAYS BEEN THE DAYTIME DRAMA QUEEN.
THE BIGGEST TV STAR THE WORLD HAS SEEN.
IT'S NOT TOO LATE
TO GET IT BACK.

I'M GONNA FIND OUT WHAT WENT WRONG AND THEN
I'LL RULE THE NEILSON RATINGS ONCE AGAIN.
YES, JUST YOU WAIT.
I'LL GET IT BACK.

I'M THE ONE WHO OUSTED POOR OLD OPRAH
AND MASSACRED MONTEL.
I BEAT THE PANTS OFF
SALLY JESSE RAPHAEL.
I HOISTED OUT GERALDO
AND SPRINGER GOT SPRUNG TOO.
AND NOW THIS COUPLES COURT SHOW
I'M COMING FOR YOU.

I'LL SIT ATOP THE LEGAL TV WORLD.
THERE ON MY THRONE, MY REGAL ROBES UNFURLED.
YES, SOMEDAY SOON
I'LL GET IT BACK.

YES, JACKIE'S COMEBACK HAS AT LAST BEGUN.
I WILL NOT STOP UNTIL I'M NUMBER ONE.
AND THERE I'LL BE
WITH EMMY TWENTY THREE.
I GUARANTEE,
I'LL GET IT BACK.
JUST WATCH AND SEE,
I'LL GET IT BACK.

>   (**HENRY** *reenters.*)

[MUSIC NO. 04A: "JUDGE JACKIE REPRISE #1"]

HENRY. All rise. This court is now in session. The Honorable Judge Jackie Justice presiding.

JACKIE/AUDIENCE.
>   JUDGE JACKIE JUSTICE.
>   JUDGE JACKIE JUSTICE.
>   JUDGE JACKIE JUSTICE.
>   JUDGE JACKIE JUSTICE.

>   (*Enter* **DUANE** *and* **LUANNE**, *two shabbily dressed rednecks.*)

HENRY. This is the plaintiff, Luanne Pumkinblotch. She claims that the defendant misappropriated their collective life savings. She is suing for two hundred dollars. This is the defendant, Duane Duaneson. He claims that *The Dukes of Hazard* is the greatest television series of all time.

DUANE. Hey Mama!

HENRY. We now call to order The Case of the Peppered Preppers.

JACKIE. Ms. Pumkinblotch?

LUANNE. Huh?

JACKIE. "Huh" is not an answer.

LUANNE. Yer-huh?

JACKIE. What is your relationship with the defendant?

DUANE. She's my womern, yer Honor.

LUANNE. Nuh-uh. I dumped yer sorry behind.

DUANE. Well, I doesn't accept.

LUANNE. Y'all doesn't have to accept.

JACKIE. And I find myself in the midst of another walking advertisement for celibacy.

LUANNE. Say wut?

JACKIE. You and the defendant were cohabitating at the time of the alleged incident?

LUANNE. Co-wut?

JACKIE. Am I speaking Swahili here? Were you living together?

LUANNE. Oh yeah. We got us a nice double wide right there on my grandaddy's pumpkin farm, between the meth lab and the other meth lab, so's we could save all a our money fer –

DUANE. Luanne, what is y'all –

JACKIE. Clam it, Cletus. You'll get your turn.

    (To **LUANNE.***)*

When did you notice that your money was missing?

LUANNE. Oh. It weren't missin'. I knowed right where it gone.

    [MUSIC NO. 05: "AIN'T NO DRILL PART I"]

    (We hear flashback music as the flashback begins.)

It wuz 'bout three o'clock in the mornin'. I knowed cuz my favorite infomercial had jist 'bout finshed up. The one fer the knives wut slice bananas real good. That's when it happened.

    (She enters the flashback.)

Wake up, Duane! Git yer lazy bones outta bed.

DUANE. Wut is it? What's the sitch-e-ation?

LUANNE.

    GO GIT YER GUN.

DUANE. My gun?

LUANNE.
GO GIT YER GUN.

DUANE. I got it.

LUANNE.
DON'T BE AN IJIT, NOT THAT GUN, GO GIT THE WAY BIGGER
ONE.
AND THEM GRENADES.

DUANE. Grenades?

LUANNE.
YEAH, THEM GRENADES.

DUANE. Which grenades?

LUANNE.
THE ONES WE KEEP THERE 'NEATH OUR PILLOW, CASE THE
GUV'MENT INVADES.
Y'ALL GOT YER KNIFE?

DUANE. The guv'ment?

LUANNE.
YER BIG ASS KNIFE.

DUANE. The guv'ment's here?

LUANNE.
YER GONNA NEED IT, YEAH, YOU BET YER WORTHLESS LIFE.
SO GIT YER GUN AND HIDE THE STILL!
THIS AIN'T NO DRILL!

DUANE. Wut we gonna do, Luanne?

LUANNE.
WE GOTTA GIT TO THAT THERE BUNKER Y'ALL BILT.
THE ONE WUT I DONE TOLE YA TA BUILD.
THANK GOD WE BILT THAT BUNKER AND FILLED IT ALL UP,
NOW LET'S NOT STOP 'TIL THAT WHOLE GUV'MENT IS
KILLED.

DUANE. Yeah, bout that bunker, Luanne –

LUANNE.
CUZ IT IS ON.

DUANE. It's jist –

LUANNE.

> THEY'S ON OUR LAWN.
> THE BIGGEST GUV'MENT POSSE THAT YOU EVER SAWN.
> SO GIT YER GUN AND FIRE AT WILL!
> THIS AIN'T NO DRILL!

Cover me –

DUANE. Luanne!

> *(She runs.)*

Noooooooooooooooooooooo!

> *(**LUANNE** gets shot by an invisible horde of government agents. She crumples to the floor. **DUANE** cradles her.)*

LUANNE. They got me, Duane. Them guv'ment bastards got me.

DUANE. Hang on, Luanne. Hang on!

LUANNE. Jist git me ta that there bunker, Duane. Git me ta that there bunker.

DUANE. Yeah, the thing bout that there bunker is –

LUANNE.

> CUZ IN OUR BUNKER,
> OUR DOOMSDAY BUNKER,
> WE'LL LIVE IN PARADISE BETWEEN THEM CONCRETE
>   WALLS.
> WE'LL HAVE SOME FLASHLIGHTS.
> AND CANNED TOMATOES.
> WE'LL EAT MARSHMALLOW PEEPS WHILE CIV'LIZATION
>   FALLS.

DUANE. Oh, Luanne.

> *(**DUANE** looks around.)*

Uh, Luanne?

LUANNE. Wut?

DUANE. That ain't no guv'ment. That there's a pumpkin patch.

LUANNE. Well, of course it's a pumpkin patch. This were a drill.

DUANE. But y'all said, "This ain't no drill."

LUANNE. Wut would we would say if it weren't no drill, huh? We'd say, "This ain't no drill." So that's wut we gotta say when it are a drill.

DUANE. I reckon, it's jist…

[MUSIC NO. 05A: "AIN'T NO DRILL PART 2"]

LUANNE. Great balls 'a fire, Duane, a zombie!

DUANE. Great balls 'a fire!

LUANNE. It's the zombie 'pocalypse, Duane. I done tole y'all it were comin'. And now here it be.

DUANE. Watch out, Luanne!

LUANNE. HE GOT MY ARM.

DUANE. I'll save y'all.

LUANNE.
SOUND THE ALARM.
WHERE IS THE FENCE WUT I DONE TOLE YOU TO BUILD
ALL ROUND THE FARM?

THIS HERE UNDEAD.
WILL EAT MY HEAD.
UNLESS Y'ALL FILL HIS ZOMBIE GUTS ALL FULL A
BUCKSHOT AND LEAD.

HE'LL EAT MY BRAINS.

DUANE. I'm comin', Luanne.

LUANNE.
DRINK FROM MY VEINS.
THEN MAKE A BIG OLE ZOMBIE MEAL A MY REMAINS.
SO GIT YER GUN AND SHOOT TA KILL.
THIS AIN'T NO DRILL!

DUANE. I'll save y'all, Luanne. Jist tell me wut ta do.

LUANNE.
IF WE COULD JIST GIT TA THAT BUNKER YA BILT.
WE COULD SHOW THEM ZOMBIES WE'S TOUGH.

LUANNE. *(cont.)*

> CUZ WE WOULD BE THERE SAFELY EATEN THEM PEEPS
> WHILE ALL THE WORLD GITS ATE BY ZOMBIES 'N' STUFF.
> Y'ALL BETTER RACE.

DUANE. It's jist –

LUANNE.

> TA GIT MY MACE.

DUANE. Ya see –

LUANNE.

> AND BLAST THIS ZOMBIE BASTARD IN HIS STUPID FACE.
> IT'S TIME FER ZOMBIE BLOOD TA SPILL.
> THIS AIN'T NO DRILL!

> Sweet mother of mercy, Duane. He bit me! He bit me, and then he sat back down. But he definitely bit me first. I'm done fer.

DUANE. Oh, Luanne.

LUANNE. Tell me 'bout that there bunker, Duane.

DUANE. See, Luanne, now that y'all mention it, there is something I been meanin' ta tell y'all bout that there bunker.

LUANNE. The light's fadin', Duane. Tell me how it's gone be.

DUANE.

> WELL, IN THAT BUNKER,
> THE ONE I BILT Y'ALL,
> THE ONE WUT DEFINITELY ISN'T BILT ON LIES.
> WE'LL HAVE SOME FLASHLIGHTS.
> AND CANNED TOMATOES.
> WE'LL EAT MARSHMALLOW PEEPS WHILE EVERYBODY DIES.

LUANNE. Oh, Duane. It's beautiful.

DUANE. Yeah, it's jist –

LUANNE. Great Xantos on High, Duane. It's the Great Xantos on High.

DUANE. Great Xantos on High! It is the Great Xantos on High.

JACKIE. What the hell is the Great Xantos on High?

LUANNE. Y'all know, the Great Xantos on High, Almighty Ruler wut created the world in two and a half hours, 'n' requires that we wear pointy hats, so's that when he returns to destroy the world in wind 'n' fire, we kin join him up there on Planet Xanotopia, jist like them prophets Jethro and Tull said.

JACKIE. And am I to understand that the two of you run practice drills to prepare for the possibility that this Xantos shows up on your front lawn?

DUANE. Well, sure.

LUANNE. Only this weren't no drill. He were there.

JACKIE. Of course he were.

LUANNE. *(She selects an audience member.)* Y'all mind standin' in fer him? Y'all look kinda Xantos-y.

> *(She helps him onto stage.)*

There he wuz, the Great Xantos on High in all his glory. And by "all his glory", I mean a **[Slightly Judgmental Assessment Of Whatever Audience Member Is Wearing]**. And he opened up his mouth, and he spaketh unto us.

XANTOS.
> IT IS I!
> THE GREAT XANTOS ON HIGH.

LUANNE. Yup. His mouth was moving all outta sync with the words like that, and he says…

XANTOS.
> I SHALT DESTROYETH THOSE WHO'VE SINNED AGAINST ME,
> LIKE ALL THOSE LUTHERANS,
> AND SILLY EPISCOPALIANS,
> AND ALL LEFTHANDED BUDDHISTS,
> AND MORMONS, AND SLUTS, AND GINGERS,
> AND FANS OF THE **[RIVAL SPORTS FRANCHISE]**,
> AND DAVID HASSELHOFF.

LUANNE. Yeah, the great Xantos on high hates David Hasselhoff. And then he says…

XANTOS.
> BUT ALL YE,
> MY CHOSEN BROTHERS AND SISTERS,

XANTOS. *(cont.)*
> WHO HEARD OF MY COMING AND BELIEVED IT,
> AND BUILT UP THY DOOMSDAY BUNKERS,
> TO ESCAPE THE APOCALYPTIC STORMS OF GODLY WIND
>   AND FIRE,
> YE SHALL BE SAVED.
> AND ALSO,
> A MESSAGE FOR THE GUY IN THE FIRST ROW,
> MASTURBATION IS A SIN.

LUANNE. And jist like that, he wuz gone. And I says…

(Snaps back into flashback.)

Duane! Duane! Wut is y'all waitin' fer? Let's git to that there bunker wut y'all bilt fer me 'fore the Great Xantos on High destroys the world in wind 'n' fire.

DUANE. Yeah. Okay, Luanne. Let's git to that there bunker.

LUANNE. And that's when I seen it, yer Honor.

JACKIE. That's when you seen what?

LUANNE.
> THERE WEREN'T NO BUNKER.
> DUANE NEVER BILT ONE.
> THAT STUPID IJIT IS A DIRTY FILTHY LIAR.
> HE STOLE MY MONEY,
> AND BILT A SPACESHIP.
> AND NOW WE'ZE GONNA GIT DESTROYED IN WIND 'N' FIRE!

DUANE. Y'all know wut? If y'all hadn't a been dumb 'nuff to smash up my spaceship real good, I'd take that spaceship and fly off to someplace far, like Mars or **[Nearby Bucolic Town With Amusing Name]**, jist so's I kin git away from y'all.

LUANNE. Y'all better fly that spaceship straight up Uranus, Duane, cuz that's 'bout as far as yer gone git bein' too dumb to figger out a way to launch it.

JACKIE. I have never, in my life, seen two people more ill-suited for one another, more ill-equipped to participate in an adult relationship, or more likely to exacerbate one another's dangerously paranoid delusions.

DUANE. Thank y'all, yer Honor.

LUANNE. That's mighty kind.

JACKIE. No. It is not mighty kind. But I'll tell you what is mighty kind, I am going to make sure that the two of y'all never see one another again.

LUANNE. Say wut?

JACKIE. I am hereby issuing a restraining order on each of you.

DUANE. Y'all cain't do that. We'ze in love!

JACKIE. You know something? People wouldn't realize what a moron you were if you kept your mouth shut, you ever heard that before? Neither did I, I just made it up. I'm gonna put it on t-shirts and make a million dollars. Henry, you want to buy a t-shirt?

HENRY. No, your Honor.

JACKIE. Right, because you're not an absolute imbecile like Romeo and Juliet over here. Love. Bah. Love'll make fools of them all, Henry. Everyone but you and me.

[MUSIC NO. 06: "IF YOU ONLY KNEW"]

HENRY.
> IF YOU ONLY KNEW
> THE SECRETS I'VE BEEN HIDING.
> IF YOU COULD SEE THROUGH
> TO THE TRUTH I'VE KEPT INSIDE.
> WHEN I LOOK AT YOU, SEDUCTIVELY PRESIDING...
> OH WHAT WOULD YOU DO
> IF YOU ONLY KNEW?

JACKIE. Let me tell you something, you castoff from the cast of *Deliverance*, on your best day, you aren't half as smart as I'll be three days after I'm dead.

HENRY.
> YOU HAVE GOT THIS WIT
> THAT I'M UTTERLY DISARMED BY.
> YOUR SARCASTIC LAUGH,
> IT SETS MY HEART ON FIRE.
> AND I MUST ADMIT, I FIND MYSELF QUITE CHARMED BY
> YOUR CYNICAL WORLDVIEW.
> IF YOU ONLY KNEW.

JACKIE. My mother used to say "Beauty fades, but stupid is forever."

LUANNE. Y'all cain't –

JACKIE. Zip it, Pumpkinbrain. I'm talking to this nimrod over here now.

HENRY.

YOU SHOW THE WORLD THE STERN AND SOBER JUDGE.
I SEE THE GIRL THAT THEY DON'T SEE.
YOU SAY IT TAKES A FOOL TO FALL IN LOVE.
WELL, MAYBE THE REAL FOOL IS ME.

IF YOU ONLY KNEW
HOW A LOOK FROM YOU COULD PLEASE ME.
HOW I TRULY LIVE
FOR THAT WRY SARDONIC SMILE.
WHAT I WOULDN'T GIVE TO FIND OUT THAT WHEN YOU
    TEASE ME
YOU'RE SAYING "I LOVE YOU."
IF YOU ONLY KNEW.

JACKIE. Henry, you want to quit daydreaming and get these idiots out of here? You look like a love-sick moron.

HENRY.

IF YOU ONLY KNEW.

JACKIE. The restraining orders go into effect immediately. You've been burned, and we're adjourned.

(**HENRY** ushers them out.)

HENRY. We're clear. That's a ten, your Honor.

JACKIE. Thank you, Henry.

(**HENRY** exits. Enter **SHANE.**)

[MUSIC NO. 06A: "SHANE'S ENTRANCE #2"]

SHANE. Jackie-ree, a word?

JACKIE. For you, Shane, I can think of two words.

SHANE. The numbers are in, Jackie-pie, and they have made it crystal clear that, in addition to celebrities, there is one thing *Celebrity Couples Court* has that your show severely lacks.

JACKIE. How can you have those numbers already?

SHANE. We don't have time to wait until we've aired something to know how it did. We need to know how it did before it did it. Yes? So, we find an audience member who represents average America, the most bland, run of the mill, commonplace human being we can find. Say, for instance…

> *(Selects an audience member.)*

This man. Then, we attach these electrodes to his head and monitor his responses while he watches your taping, thus deducerating exactly what everyone else in the country is going to think. We call them the… What's your name?

> *(He answers.)*

We call them the **[His Name]** Ratings. That's copyrighted, **[His Name]**. We'll sue. Allow me to demonstrate. Mr. Rogers.

> ***[MUSIC NO. 06B: "SHANE'S RATINGS"]***

> *(A series of beeps from his meter reader.)*

See? A sharp spike. Internet videos of kittens.

> *(More beeps.)*

Ah, note how the **[His Name]** Ratings skyrocket. **[Rival City]**.

> *(A series of descending beeps.)*

You see, Jackie? A perfect representation of how the entire nation feels. Now, observe. Love.

> *(The ratings skyrocket.)*

There. Love, Jackie, romance. That's what audiences want, and that's what *Celebrity Couples Court* delivers. Your show has to tell a good old-fashioned American love story.

JACKIE. We include a lot of cases like that.

SHANE. And how do they usually turn out?

JACKIE. I'm not sure what you're referring to.

SHANE. Let's take a look at a random cross-sampling from the last three years.

(He pulls out a remote, as a screen descends.)

The Case of the Dubious Donor.

[MUSIC NO. 06C: "FLASHBACK CASES"]

(JACKIE, DONOR MAN, and DONOR WOMAN enact each flashback.)

JACKIE. And exactly what is the stolen property you'd like your exwife to return?

DONOR MAN. My kidney.

DONOR WOMAN. You gave me that kidney!

DONOR MAN. I gave my wife that kidney!

DONOR WOMAN. I need that kidney!

DONOR MAN. Why don't you go get that yoga instructor's kidney?

JACKIE. I haven't seen anything this offensive since my nephew's third grade production of *Cabaret*. Ruling for the defendant. You've been burned, and we're adjourned!

(The highlight ends. Exit DONOR MAN and WOMAN.)

That is not an altogether accurate –

(Enter CATFISH GUY.)

SHANE. The Case of the Fictional Fiancee.

CATFISH GUY. I don't care if we've never met in person. I don't care if we've never talked on the phone. I don't even care that she's actually a fictitious online persona invented by two high school sophomores. I love her!

JACKIE. Love makes less sense than male nipples. Ruling for the defendant. You've been burned, and we're adjourned!

(The highlight ends. Exit CATFISH GUY.)

Shane, you have to take into account the fact that –

(Enter BUILDING LADY.)

SHANE. The Case of the Monumental Molester.

BUILDING LADY. You don't understand, I am in love with the Washington Monument. I can't help it if the physical expression of it makes some people uncomfortable.

JACKIE. I may love Rocky Road, ma'am, but I'm not about to straddle a Baskin Robbins. You've been burned, and we're adjourned.

(The highlight ends. Exit **BUILDING LADY**.*)*

Alright, I may have once or twice ruled in ways that could be interpreted as –

SHANE. The point is this: Love sells. And you'd better change your tune and let it sell this next case, Jackie-bee, or I'm afraid drastic measures will have to be taken.

(He exits.)

JACKIE. You don't think I can? You think I'm too stubborn and cynical to give one little case a happily-ever-after ending when the future of my show is at stake? You'll see. Love conquers all.

[MUSIC NO. 06D: "ALLISTER DREAM #2"]

*(***YOUNG ALLISTER** *appears.)*

YOUNG ALLISTER. It certainly does.

JACKIE. Allister?

YOUNG ALLISTER. And today, on the first anniversary of our nuptial bliss, I wanted to remind you of the permanence of our romantic relationship.

JACKIE. You were so handsome.

*(***ALLISTER** *appears, and cuts in again.)*

ALLISTER. You don't have to tell me twice.

JACKIE. No, I want to go back to –

ALLISTER. Yessir, love conquers all. That's a lesson I'm learning all over again on this honeymoon.

JACKIE. You're on another honeymoon? What, the 24 year old paralegal you ditched me for isn't doing it for you anymore?

ALLISTER. The trouble with 24-year-old paralegals is that they quickly become 25-year-old paralegals. I'm on to 23-year-old paralegals now. Would you like to meet the latest?

JACKIE. Oh, I don't think that's –

ALLISTER. Splendid. Because here she is. My saucy little minx.

(He pulls a woman from the audience.)

Come now, darling. Don't be shy. Her name is... Susan or something. Martha? Destiny? Svetlana?

(She says her name.)

[Her Name]. Of course it is, **[Her Name]**. I know that. We're married. And, Jackie?

JACKIE. Yes?

ALLISTER. Did I mention the fact that she's extraordinarily flexible?

JACKIE. You didn't.

ALLISTER. Like an underfed Chinese contortionist. She can perform the most unbelievable feats of human flexibility. Go on and show her, darling...

(He encourages her to try something.)

But enough about my fulfilling sex life.

(To the audience member.)

Thank you, darling.

(To JACKIE.)

You see, Jackie? If you would just open your heart, you too can get everything you want. Right, **[Her Name]**?

(He winks at her.)

Just open the door to love, Jackie, and all your dreams will come true.

JACKIE. That's ridiculous, Allister. I don't dream about trumped-up Hallmark emotions. Never have, never will.

[MUSIC NO. 06E: "JORGE DE AMOR"]

(He disappears. Enter **JORGE DE AMOR**, *an over the top Telemundo stereotype played by* **HENRY**.*)*

JORGE. Never, *Señora?*

JACKIE. I beg your pardon.

JORGE. I say, never, *Señora?*

JACKIE. Who the hell are you?

JORGE. Ah, *Señora*, how quickly chu forget. It is I, Jorge de Amor.

JACKIE. Jorge de Amor?

JORGE. Sí. Jorge de Amor.

JACKIE. Jorge de Amor was a fictional character on a telenovela I watched in middle school.

JORGE. Si, Señora. Chu remember. All those afternoons we spend together. Chour *madre*, off at work, chour *padre*, *Dios* know where, y chu, unable afford the American shows, curled up on the couch with Jorge de Amor, a poor Mexican revolutionary who chuses his law degree to fight for truth, justice, y…*de amor.*

(We see **YOUNG JACKIE** *in front of the TV.* **YOUNG JORGE** *appears.)*

YOUNG JORGE. *Muchachas y muchachos* of the yury. Do chu believe in truth?

YOUNG JACKIE. I believe in truth.

YOUNG JORGE. Do chu believe in justice?

YOUNG JACKIE. I believe in justice.

YOUNG JORGE. Then chu must find the law degree-wielding revolutionary in chour heart, y chu must fight!

YOUNG JACKIE. Oh Jorge…

YOUNG JORGE. The people, they rest, chour Honor.

YOUNG JACKIE. *Te adoro.*

ALL FOUR. JORGE DE AMOR!

*(***YOUNG JACKIE** *and* **YOUNG JORGE** *disappear.)*

JACKIE. That was a long time ago. I don't buy into that nonsense now.

JORGE. *Y* chet, here I am.

JACKIE. Get out of my head, Jorge.

JORGE. Oh, Senora. There are things in chour head that chu do no even know that chu know, chu know?

JACKIE. What are you talking about?

[MUSIC #07: "CHOUR FANTASY"]

JORGE.

> WELL, CHOUR HEAD DOES NO KNOW.
> WHAT GO ON IN CHOUR HEAD.
> IF CHU THINK THAT CHU KNOW
> CHU HAVE BEEN MISLED.

> CHU HAVE NEEDS Y DESIRES
> YOU SUPPRESS Y DENY.
> BUT CHOU'LL NEVER EXTINGUISH CHOUR FIRES
> EVEN IF CHOU TRY.

> NOW CHOU'RE HERE WHERE CHOUR DREAMS ARE SET
>   FREE:
> CHOUR FANTASY.

JACKIE. I do not fantasize about a television character from my adolescence.

JORGE. Perhaps then there is someone who remind you of Jorge, hm?

JACKIE. What?

JORGE. Someone who, like Jorge, help chu in chour pursuit of truth, justice, *y de amor.*

JACKIE. I do not think of anyone this way.

> (**JORGE** *snaps his fingers.* **JACKIE,** *unable to control herself, begins to dance with him.*)

JORGE.

> CHU MAY SAY CHU NO THINK,
> BUT CHOUR TRUE FEELINGS SHOW.
> THEY HIDE WHERE CHU NO SEE,
> BURIED DOWN BELOW.

> BUT WHEN THAT TANGO START,
> AND CHU DANCE JUST LIKE THIS,

> WELL, THE MUSIC BEGIN IN CHOUR HEART,
> ENDING IN A KISS.
>
> SI, CHOU'RE HERE WHERE CHOUR DREAMS COME TO BE:
> CHOUR FANTASY.

JACKIE. I haven't danced with anyone since…well, in a long time.

JORGE. This is too bad, *Señora*.

JACKIE. But there's a reason for that.

JORGE. Oh?

JACKIE.

> MUSIC CAN SHAKE YOU.
> MUSIC CAN TAKE YOU
> STRAIGHT TO THE TALL MOUNTAINTOPS.
>
> OH HOW IT THRILLS YOU,
> SAVES AND FULFILLS YOU,
> YES, BUT IT KILLS WHEN IT STOPS.
>
> IT ALWAYS STOPS.

JORGE. Perhaps chu are right. But, perhaps chu are wrong, no?

> MAYBE ONE DAY THIS WON'T ONLY BE
> CHOUR FANTASY.

JACKIE. What are you talking about?

JORGE.

> IF CHU WANT CHOUR FANTASY
> FOR TO BE REALITY
> CHU MUST SAY *SÍ*.

JACKIE.

> I MUST SAY *SÍ?*

JORGE.

> CHU JUST SAY *SÍ*.

JACKIE.

> I MUST SAY *SÍ?*

JORGE.

> SAY *SÍ*.

JACKIE.
SÍ?

JORGE.
SÍ.

JACKIE.
SI.

JORGE.
SI.

JACKIE.
SI.

JORGE.
SI.

JACKIE.
SI.

JACKIE. *Sí. Sí. Dios mio, mi corazón dice en Espagnol perfecto, mil veces sí.*

> *(The fantasy ends and the lights shift as **JORGE** becomes **HENRY**.)*

HENRY. See what?

JACKIE. Hm? Henry? Henry! Oh. Henry. I didn't hear you come in, Henry.

HENRY. You said, "see."

JACKIE. You must have been imagining things, Henry.

HENRY. Yes, your Honor.

JACKIE. Very dangerous, imagining.

HENRY. Yes, your Honor.

JACKIE. Oftentimes your mind makes you imagine things that in reality you would never, ever consider a remote possibility because they are completely ridiculous and absurd and certainly not representative of what you are actually thinking or feeling.

HENRY. Your Honor?

JACKIE. This is the longest ten minute break I've ever experienced.

> *(She exits.)*

[MUSIC. NO. 08: "LIKE YOUR MOTHER DOES"]

HENRY. Your Honor, wait. I wanted to explain what a suitable romantic partner I would... Oh, who are you kidding, Henry? You're pathetic.

(**HENRY**'s **MOTHER** *appears.*)

MAMA. Watch it, mister. That's my son you're talking about.

HENRY. Mama? What are you doing here?

MAMA. I'm your mother, Henry, I'm always looking out for you, even in your subconscious. Now, what seems to be the problem?

HENRY. It's nothing.

MAMA. Are the other children mocking your abnormally large ears?

HENRY. No, it's not – I have abnormally large ears?

MAMA. No.

HENRY. The thing is, there's this girl...

MAMA. Oh my.

HENRY. Mama...

MAMA. Oh, Henry. I'm just so happy. After all these years, and with how sensitive you are, and the figure skating lessons, your father and I thought...well, never you mind what we thought. Tell me about this girl. She's not fast, is she?

HENRY. No, Mama, she's –

MAMA. 'Cause that Remy McNichols next door was fast, and you know what happened to her.

HENRY. Mama, she –

MAMA. Dead. Shark attack. I'm just saying.

HENRY. I'm not certain she likes me.

MAMA. What's not to like?

YOU'RE A FASCINATING BOY, HENRY.
CHARMING AND WELL-READ.
YOU'RE TALENTED AND SMART,
YES, DESPITE WHAT ALL YOUR TEACHERS SAID.

HENRY. What did my teachers say?

MAMA.

> YOU'RE A VERY LOVELY BOY, HENRY.
> ELEGANT AND CLEAN.
> THE GIRLS ARE BOUND TO WANT A KISS,
> SO MAYBE TRY SOME LISTERINE.
>
> AND WHEN THEY FLOCK TO YOU,
> JUST KEEP YOUR HEAD BECAUSE
> NOBODY LOVES YOU
> LIKE YOUR MOTHER DOES.

HENRY. That's a terribly depressing thought, Mama.

MAMA.

> YOU'RE A VERY MANLY BOY, HENRY.
> SEE HOW STRONG YOU'VE GROWN.
> YOU'RE INDEPENDENT TOO
> SINCE YOU'RE FORTY-THREE AND ALL ALONE.
>
> YOU'VE NEVER BEEN TO JAIL, HENRY.
> THAT SHOWS YOU HAVE CLASS.
> NOW, LET'S JUST HOPE THE GIRLS DON'T CARE
> ABOUT YOUR AWFUL NIGHTTIME GAS.
>
> THE MAN I SEE TODAY
> IS NOT THE BOY HE WAS.
> NOBODY LOVES YOU
> LIKE YOUR MOTHER DOES.

Now go on.

HENRY. What?

MAMA. Pretend I'm this harlot of Babylon of yours.

HENRY. Absolutely not.

MAMA. How are you going to gain confidence if you don't practice?

HENRY. Hello –

MAMA. What's wrong with your face?

HENRY. What? What are you talking about?

MAMA. What if she asks that?

HENRY. I –

MAMA. Is that your face, or did your neck throw up?

HENRY. Is she going to say that?

MAMA. How would I know?

HENRY. I –

MAMA. You're ugly.

HENRY. I give up.

MAMA.

> HENRY, I TRIED TO RAISE YOU TO BE CONFIDENT.
> SO THAT YOUR SELF-ESTEEM WOULD TAKE YOU FAR.
>
> IF YOU ONLY BELIEVE THAT YOU ARE GOOD ENOUGH,
> YOU WON'T SCREW UP LIKE THE SCREW UP THAT YOU ARE.
> YOU ARE A VERY HANDSOME BOY, HENRY.
> DAPPER, DEBONAIR.
> YOU LOOK JUST LIKE BRAD PITT.
> IF HE GAINED SOME WEIGHT AND QUEERED HIS HAIR.
>
> YOU'LL FIND A LOVELY GIRL, HENRY.
> PUT YOUR MIND AT EASE.
> AND I JUST PRAY THAT SHE WON'T MIND
> YOUR GENITAL DEFORMITIES.
>
> AND IF THAT HUSSY MINDS,
> WELL, YOU JUST DROP THAT SCUZ,
> NOBODY LOVES YOU.
> I'M SAYING NOBODY LOVES YOU.
> OH HENRY, NOBODY LOVES YOU…

HENRY. Mama?

MAMA. Hm?

HENRY. Were you going to finish that thought?

MAMA. What thought?

> *(She exits.* **HENRY** *sighs. Enter* **SHANE** *and* **JACKIE.***)*

SHANE. Good news, Jackie-kins, I reached out to Britley Spanx's people and they're interested.

JACKIE. The teen drama queen? We talked about this –

SHANE. She is not currently in jail, and is in the midst of kicking a killer glue-sniffing habit.

JACKIE. Shane –

SHANE. High possibility for drama, that's all I'm saying.

JACKIE. Read my lips, Shane. The only way some privileged, plastic princess is going to prance around here with a tiny, jewel-encrusted dog in her purse is over my dead body.

> *[MUSIC NO. 08A: "JUDGE JACKIE REPRISE #2"]*

SHANE. Well then, let's make sure we end this case with a good-old-fashioned-love-conquers-all-happily-ever-after-ride-into-the-sunset, shall we?

HENRY. All rise. This court is once again in session.

JACKIE/AUDIENCE.

> JUDGE JACKIE JUSTICE.
> JUDGE JACKIE JUSTICE.
> JUDGE JACKIE JUSTICE.
> JUDGE JACKIE JUSTICE.

> *(Enter* **TREAT** *and* **POO-BEAR**.*)*

HENRY. This is the plaintiff, "Treat" Macklin. He claims that the defendant owes him money for an unfinished artwork. He is suing for one thousand dollars.

TREAT. Boom!

HENRY. This is the defendant, "Poo-Bear" Daniels. She claims that, for all she cares, the plaintiff can pay for his own damn artwork. We now call to order The Case of I Tawt I Taw a Titty Tat.

JACKIE. And we're right back into the fray. Mr. Macklin?

TREAT. Sup?

JACKIE. Sup is not a word in any language I'm familiar with.

TREAT. Das how it be on the street.

JACKIE. You're from the street?

TREAT. Word.

JACKIE. Your home address is listed as 42 Apple Blossom Way.

TREAT. Apple Blossom Way be the baddest cul de sac in **[Local Well-To-Do, Extremely White Neighborhood]**.

JACKIE. Take your hat off, pull your pants up, and get back to waiting for the Funky Bunch to arrive, Melvin.

POO-BEAR. Ha. She call you Melvin.

TREAT. Yo, das not my name.

POO-BEAR. Melvin.

TREAT. My name Treat. E'rybody know dat.

JACKIE. And why do they call you Treat, Melvin?

TREAT. They call me Treat cuz I be all…dag, psssh, like blam! Just like…boom! When I do my thang, you know?

JACKIE. Yes, I understand perfectly. And Miss…Poo-Bear, you dated M.C. Country Club here?

POO-BEAR. What happened was my cousin, she say I gots to come down Pottery Barn, right? cuz they gots these stupid-fly new duvet covers that I just gots to check out.

(Their flashback begins.)

And there he be.

TREAT. Damn girl. Yo, you gots to check out them stupid-fly new duvet covers we just gots in.

JACKIE. *(Cutting off the flashback.)* If I wanted to hear somebody ramble on about things I don't care about, I'd ask my brother-in-law about his fantasy football team. All I want to know is whether or not you entered into a romantic relationship.

POO-BEAR. I guess.

JACKIE. Why are you claiming she owes you a thousand dollars?

TREAT. She make me get a tat.

JACKIE. A what?

HENRY. A tattoo, your Honor.

JACKIE. Thank you, Henry. You made him get a tattoo?

POO-BEAR. Yeah.

JACKIE. Why?

POO-BEAR. He my boo.

JACKIE. Your what?

POO-BEAR. My boo.

HENRY. Her boyfriend, your Honor.

JACKIE. What was the tattoo?

POO-BEAR. My name.

JACKIE. You wanted him to get Poo-Bear permanently printed on his chest in case, what, you forgot which privileged semiliterate wannabe gangster was your boyfriend?

TREAT. Ha. She be sayin' you stupid.

JACKIE. Melvin, your speaking privileges are revoked until you learn to conjugate a verb.

POO-BEAR. I be wantin' him to get it so all them dirty skanks down Pottery Barn know he mine.

JACKIE. A logical course of action.

POO-BEAR. Thank you.

JACKIE. So, she paid for the tattoo that you agreed to have inked into your own skin?

POO-BEAR. Das exactly how it happen.

TREAT. Naw. Naw. Naw she ain't.

JACKIE. Alright, Melvin. Then tell me how it did happen.

[MUSIC NO. 09: "POOB!"]

TREAT.
> YO, YO, YO. HERE BE WHAT I'M SAYIN':
> SHE TELL ME GET THE TAT, AND SHE PROMISE SHE BE PAYIN'.
> SHE WANT TO BE MY GURL, YEAH, SHE WANT TO WEAR MY RANG,
> BUT SHE AIN'T DONE PAID FOR THE WHOLE DAMN THANG.

POO-BEAR. Das cuz you ain't gots the whole thang, does you, Treat?

TREAT. Naw, das my point. I ain't.

JACKIE. You never got the whole tattoo?

TREAT. Naw.

POO-BEAR. Yeah, cuz you be leavin' my cousin tattoo parlor to go get all up on that skank Charlotta down Panera Bread.

JACKIE. What happened?

TREAT.

> I WENT TO POO-BEAR COUSIN, HE SAY I SHOULD BE SEATED,
> HE STARTED ON HER NAME, BUT HE NEVER DONE
>   COMPLETED.
> NOW I TAKE MY SHIRT OFF, AND E'RYBODY LAUGH.
> I AIN'T GOTS THE WHOLE TATTOO, I ONLY GOTS HALF.

JACKIE. So, what you're telling me is –

TREAT. Boom!

> *(He rips off his shirt.)*

It say Poob!

JACKIE. It says what?

TREAT.

> GIRL, POOB!
> I GOTS POOB ON MY CHEST.
> DAS A PRETTY STUPID WORD TO BE WRITTEN ON YOUR
>   BREAST.
>
> POOB!
> I GOTS POOB ON MY CHEST.
> I SHOW IT TO THE HUNNIES, BUT THEY ISN'T TOO
>   IMPRESSED.
>
> POOB!
> I GOTS POOB ON MY CHEST.
> NOW THE GIRLS BE ALL SNICKERIN' WHENEVER I'S
>   UNDRESSED.
> POOB!
> I GOTS POOB ON MY CHEST.
> AND NOW I BE ALL GROUNDED CUZ I FAILED MY ENGLISH
>   TEST.
>
> POOB!

JACKIE. And the wonders of the human fallacy known as love continue to amaze.

(Beat.)

Nevertheless, due to certain extenuating circumstances, it might, perhaps, be worth considering the possibility that a solution might be found where these two can work out their differences and learn to once again... uhm...

[MUSIC NO. 09A: "ALLISTER APPEARS"]

(Enter **ALLISTER**.)

ALLISTER. 'Atta girl, Jackie.

JACKIE. Allister? What...what are you –

ALLISTER. Just mend the fences between these two love birds, prove the neverending power of love, and your dreams of getting back on top can all come true.

JACKIE. The power of love, huh?

ALLISTER. Look what it did for us.

JACKIE. You stole my idea, my show, and you perverted it, turned it into that celebrity couple nonsense.

ALLISTER. That's exactly my point.

JACKIE. What are you talking about?

ALLISTER. If you hadn't fallen for me, I would never have been able to do any of that.

(He disappears.)

HENRY. Your Honor?

JACKIE. Hm?

HENRY. We're still rolling.

JACKIE. What's that?

HENRY. Did you want to issue a verdict?

JACKIE. I did, Henry. I did want to issue a verdict. Consider yourselves lucky that it is beyond the scope of my office to sentence you to enforced sterilization. As it is, I will do whatever is in my power to ensure that the travesty of your romantic involvement never occurs again. You've both been burned, and we're adjourned.

> *(They exit. Enter* **SHANE.***)*

SHANE. Not exactly the ride into the sunset we were looking for.

JACKIE. You couldn't possibly expect me to –

SHANE. Bring the sign in.

[MUSIC NO. 09B: "BRING THE SIGN IN"]

> *(A new sign is flown in. It's neon, flashy, and all kinds of garish.)*

JACKIE. What the –

SHANE. And hit the lights!

> *(The lights shift to a much flashier design, including a disco ball.)*

JACKIE. What is the meaning of –

SHANE. And get the mud wrestling pit!

> *(He snaps his fingers.)*

JACKIE. This is my show. I'm the executive producer –

[MUSIC NO. 10: "NOT ME"]

SHANE. You should reacquaint yourself with your contract, Jackie-pie. If at any point the **[His Name]*** ratings fall below a two point oh, which, thanks to your most recent tirade, they have, the network can exercise its right to claim final say over all design decisions.

JACKIE. You set me up.

HENRY. The ratings are down?

JACKIE. You knew I'd never rule in favor of reuniting those two –

---

* Name of rating first established previously in Act I with male audience member (first appears on page 31 of script).

SHANE. It's this or cancellation.

HENRY. Cancellation?

SHANE. Of course, these are purely the superfluicial changes. The most important thing to keep in mind is that in every single case that goes on the air, love must win in the end, or your little show decidedly won't.

(**SHANE** *exits.*)

HENRY. Oh dear. Cancellation? In light of that, your Honor, there is something that I need to tell you. Or, ask you, I suppose. I mean... Your Honor, would you like to, that is, for many years, I've... What I'm trying to say is –

JACKIE.

DO YOU KNOW WHAT I THINK, HENRY?

I THINK LOVE IS FOR SUCKERS, AND SAPS AND MORONIC IDIOTS

SO DRUNK ON THEIR DAMN FAIRY TALES THAT THEY'RE DRIVEN HALF INSANE.

HENRY. Oh.

JACKIE.

DO YOU KNOW SOMETHING ELSE, HENRY?

I THINK IF YOU'RE IN LOVE YOU DESERVE TO BE TAKEN OUT AND SHOT.

'CAUSE YOU HAVE BEEN DOOMED TO A LIFE FULL OF MISERY AND PAIN.

BUT NOT ME.

NO, NOT ME.

I AM NOT THAT NAIVE.

SAVE YOUR STORYBOOK ENDINGS FOR THOSE DUMB ENOUGH TO BELIEVE.

NO, NOT ME.

NEVER ME.

'CAUSE IT'S PURE FANTASY.

YOU MAY CHOOSE TO BUY INTO A LIE THAT WILL NOT COME TO BE.

BUT NOT ME.

HENRY. Of course. Why would you ever consider… I mean, nevermind.

JACKIE.

IF I'VE LEARNED ANYTHING, HENRY,
IT'S THAT I'D RATHER PULL OUT MY TEETH WHEN MY GUMS
    AREN'T EVEN NUMB.
THAN DIE OF THE ROMANTIC PLAGUE THAT THE WHOLE
    WORLD SUFFERS FROM.

SO NOT ME.
NO, NOT ME.
I REFUSE TO TAKE PART
IN THE FATAL DISEASE THAT TAKES AIM AT THE FRAIL
    HUMAN HEART.
NO, NOT ME.
WATCH AND SEE.
YOU HAVE MY GUARANTEE.
ONE BY ONE, DAY BY DAY, THEY FALL PREY TO THIS CURSED
    MALADY.

TWENTY YEARS I'VE WATCHED AND SEEN
ALL THE THINGS THAT LOVE MIGHT MEAN:
JEALOUSY, BETRAYAL AND FRUSTRATION.

TWENTY YEARS I'VE LEARNED TOO WELL
LOVE IS BOUND TO BURN LIKE HELL,
SO I'VE BUILT THIS BLISSFUL ISOLATION.

ALL THE PAIN
THAT I'VE KNOWN
WILL NOT HURT ME WITH A HEART MADE OF STONE.
ON MY OWN
INVINCIBLE AND ALL ALONE.

SO, NOT ME.
I AM FREE
FROM THE INSANITY.
EVERY DAY I PREVAIL OVER LOVE DOOMED TO FAIL
    MISERABLY.

NO, NOT ME.
NEVER ME.

JACKIE.

IT WAS NOT MEANT TO BE.

LET THE WORLD GO TO HELL CAUGHT IN LOVE'S FIERY
SPELL,
THEY WILL ROT IN THE FLAMING DEBRIS.
BUT NOT ME.
NOT ME.

I quit!

(She storms out.)

End of Act I

ACT II

(In the darkness, we hear an overly dramatic voice over and see a revised version of JACKIE's intro video.)

SHANE. *(Voice over.)* She's the quick-witted judge whose passion for justice took her from the mean streets of Brooklyn to the highest courts in the land.

(The lights come up to reveal HENRY, in drag, behind the bench. He looks vaguely like JACKIE. SHANE holds HENRY's clipboard.)

And now, she's getting a little more funky.

[MUSIC NO. 10A: "JUDGE JACKIE (REPRISE #3)"]

HENRY. Shane –

(SHANE rips off the lower half of HENRY's robe, revealing his calves.)

SHANE. *(Voice over.)* And showing a little more skin.

(Funky music plays.)

HENRY. I'm sorry, what?

(SHANE urges HENRY to dance. He does. Very awkwardly.)

SHANE. *(Voice over.)* She's the sexy, funkified judge who loves to dance. She is... Judge Jackie Justice.

HENRY (AS JACKIE) & ALL.
JUDGE JACKIE JUSTICE.
JUDGE JACKIE JUSTICE.
JUDGE JACKIE JUSTICE.
JUDGE JACKIE –
Oh, forget it.

(Enter **KITTY***, wearing whiskers, cat ears, and a tail.)*

SHANE. This is the plaintiff, Kitty McMeow. She claims that the defendant's refusal to take off his foam anteater head has caused her severe emotional damage. She is suing for thirteen cans of tuna fish.

KITTY. Meow.

(Enter **ANTONY***, wearing a foam anteater head.)*

SHANE. This is the defendant, Antony Anteater. He claims that anteaters do not speak.

(Pause, as **ANTONY** *stares straight ahead.)*

We now call to order the Case of the Furious Furry.

HENRY. *(To* SHANE*.)* Shane, they're dressed like animals.

SHANE. I know. They're furries. They derive certain physical pleasures from dressing like anthropomogriphal animals.

HENRY. *(As* JACKIE*.)* Okay... So... Ms. McMeow?

KITTY. Meow. Antony and I met at the convention last year, and I don't think it's a stretch to say that we got along purrrrrfectly. But, I'm beginning to think that we're really two different species.

HENRY. *(As* JACKIE*.)* I see. I mean... A very sarcastic remark.

KITTY. Don't get me wrong meow, I still get sexually aroused by dressing like a cat and all, but Antony is on a whole 'nother level. He's method.

HENRY. *(As* JACKIE*.)* Mr. Anteater, what, uh, what do you have to say for yourself?

(No response.)

Yes, well, as far as I can tell, you're both morons. I'm sorry, that wasn't very polite. What I meant to say was that perhaps you could work out your differences amicably –

[MUSIC NO. 10B: "JACKIE TAKES OFF HEAD"]

(**ANTONY** *removes his foam head and costume, to reveal* JACKIE.)

JACKIE. You have got to be kidding me!

HENRY. Your Honor?

KITTY. This explains so much meow.

(*She exits.*)

HENRY. Your Honor... You're a furry?

JACKIE. Don't be ridiculous, Henry. I gave the weirdo some ants to let me borrow his costume so that I could keep an eye on what this pinhead was doing to my show.

SHANE. Correction, Jackie-cakes. It's not your show anymore.

JACKIE. My name is on it.

SHANE. The network owns your name.

JACKIE. I'm still a producer.

SHANE. But you can't exercise your produceatorial authority unless you're also the star.

JACKIE. Fine. If it prevents you from turning my show into this farcical Rupaul nightmare, then under protest, I'm back in.

[MUSIC NO. 10C: "JACKIE'S BACK IN"]

HENRY. Oh thank goodness.

JACKIE. I can't believe you were willing to subject yourself to...this.

HENRY. Well, I know how much the show means to – I mean, I...didn't want the show to get cancelled.

JACKIE. Henry, you...you...you look terrible.

SHANE. Thrilled to have you back, Jacks. And I've got the perfect case to celebrate your return.

JACKIE. Hang on. I've got a few demands to go over first –

SHANE. Demands?

JACKIE. Things are going to change around here, Shane.

SHANE. I couldn't agree more. Keep the cameras rolling. Hank?

(SHANE hands HENRY the clipboard and exits.)

HENRY. This the plaintiff, Britley Spanx.

JACKIE. Oh for the love of God.

HENRY. She claims that her father's managerial incompetence has hindered her burgeoning musical career. She is suing for emancipation.

BRITLEY. Totes.

(Enter FRANK.)

HENRY. This is the defendant, Frank Spanx. He claims that the only thing he's guilty of is fatherly love. We now call to order The Case of the Disgruntled Diva's Deadbeat Dad.

JACKIE. Henry, I may need you to hold my hair back.

(To BRITLEY.)

Miss?

BRITLEY. What?

JACKIE. The proper response is, "Yes, your Honor."

BRITLEY. Whatever.

JACKIE. I'm inclined to rule on your behalf to compensate you for the damage that must have been done by any parent who would name a child Britley.

FRANK. Objection, your Honor, we didn't name her Britley. We named her –

BRITLEY. Daddy!

FRANK. We named her Isabelle.

BRITLEY. I told you to never say that hideous name again, Daddy. God!

FRANK. I love you, pumpkin.

BRITLEY. Shut up, Daddy!

JACKIE. I'll be the one to silence people in this courtroom, Missy. Now, I understand that you are some type of musician.

BRITLEY. Totes.

JACKIE. What do you do?

BRITLEY. Duh. I do, like, super awesome hits like, "Baby, Baby, Baby," and "Ooh, Ooh, Baby, Ooh," and "Spank Me, Baby, Like a Naughty Baby Who Likes to Be Spanked."

JACKIE. My faith in the future of humanity has been restored.

HENRY. Your Honor –

JACKIE. What do you do? What instrument do you play?

BRITLEY. Duh. I sing. And I do my moves.

FRANK. You certainly do, honey.

BRITLEY. Daddy!

JACKIE. Your...moves?

BRITLEY. Uh... Yeah. I'm all...

(She gyrates.)

And then I'm all...

(More gyrations.)

And then I'm all...

(She continues gyrating.)

FRANK. You're so graceful, sweetheart.

JACKIE. If I wanted to be entertained in such a manner, I'd never miss Underage Tourette's Night at the **[Seedy Local Strip Club]**. Now, why don't you tell me why you think you should be emancipated?

BRITLEY. I think you'll understand if you listen to my new single...

JACKIE. And I once again wonder why the universe hates me.

[MUSIC NO. 11: "MY DADDY HATE ME"]

BRITLEY.
> OW OW
> OH OH
> OW OW
> OH OH
> A DADDY 'SPOSED TO LOVE HIS BABY BOO. (OOH OOH OOH)

BRITLEY. *(cont.)*

> A DADDY 'SPOSED TO MAKE HER DREAMS COME TRUE.
>> (OOH OOH OOH)
> A DADDY, HE 'SPOSED TO BE ALL SUGAR AND SPICE.
> MY DADDY'S LIKE SATAN, BUT NOT AS NICE.

BRITLEY & MEN.

> MY DADDY HATE ME.

BRITLEY.

> HE SUCH A MEANY.
> HE WILL NOT LET ME BUY ANOTHER LAMBORGHINI.
>
> OH,

BRITLEY & MEN.

> MY DADDY HATE ME.

BRITLEY.

> OH WHAT A HOSE JOB.
> HE ONLY PAID FOR HALF OF MY ELEVENTH NOSE JOB.
>
> OH,

BRITLEY & MEN.

> MY DADDY HATE ME.
> MEAN, MEAN DADDY. OH OH.
> MEAN, MEAN DADDY.

FRANK. That's terrific, sweet pea.

BRITLEY. Daddy, you're too fat to be a backup dancer!

FRANK. I'm sorry, sugar plum!

BRITLEY. Hire me a new back up dancer!

FRANK. Alright, how about…

> *(He looks through the audience for volunteers.)*

BRITLEY. No, Daddy. Someone hot.

FRANK. You sir? Come on up and dance with my little nightingale.

BRITLEY. Teach him my moves, Daddy.

FRANK. So, here you go. It's just…

> *(He shows the volunteer a simple step.)*

One. Two. Three. Four. Got it? One. Two. Three. Four.
It doesn't get any harder than this. Okay, baby, you can
go on with the second verse now. You're doing great.

BRITLEY.

A DADDY 'SPOSED TO HELP HIS CHICKADEE. (OH, THAT'S
ME)

(whispers) I HATE YOU, DADDY.

A DADDY GIVE HER WINGS AND SET HER FREE. (FREE FREE
ME)

A DADDY, HE 'SPOSED TO MAKE HIS BIRD LEARN TO FLY.

BUT MY DADDY MAKES ME LIKE WANT TO DIE.

BRITLEY & MEN.

MY DADDY HATE ME.

BRITLEY.

I'M SO DETESTED.

HE MAKE A FROWNIE FACE EACH TIME I GET ARRESTED.

BRITLEY & MEN.

OH, MY DADDY HATE ME.

BRITLEY.

HE MEAN AND SMELLY.

HE WILL NOT LET ME GO TO DINNER WITH R. KELLY.

OH,

BRITLEY & MEN.

MY DADDY HATE ME.

MEAN, MEAN DADDY. OH. OH.

MEAN, MEAN DADDY.

BRITLEY. Daddy, this backup dancer sucks. Fire him.

FRANK. Oh, but don't you think –

BRITLEY. Fire him!

FRANK. I'm terribly sorry, sir. You can sit back down now.
Was that okay, princess?

BRITLEY.

A DADDY, HE 'SPOSED TO TREAT HIS DAUGHTER HUMANE.

BUT MY DADDY'S MORE LIKE SADDAM HUSSEIN.

HE A MEAN, MEAN DADDY.

HE MEAN, MEAN DADDY.

BRITLEY. *(cont.)*

> HE SO FAKE AND FATTY.
> HE MEAN, MEAN DADDY.
>
> HE MAKE ME SO SADDY.
> HE MEAN, MEAN DADDY.
>
> HE FROM CINCINNATI.
>
> MY DADDY HATE ME.
> HE SUCH A NAZI.
> HE DOESN'T LIKE IT WHEN I FLASH THE PAPARAZZI.
>
> MY DADDY HATE ME.
> THAT SOCIAL CRIPPLE.
> HE GETS ALL SNIPPY IF I EVEN SLIP A NIPPLE.
>
> OH, MY DADDY HATE ME.
> OH OH OH OH OH.
> MY DADDY HATE ME.
>
> MY DADDY HATE ME.
> HE'S SUCH A NAZI.
> HE DOESN'T LIKE IT WHEN I FLASH THE PAPARAZZI.
>
> MY DADDY HATE ME.

That song was called "My Daddy Hate Me Semicolon Mean, Mean Daddy Exclamation Point Parentheses Baby".

JACKIE. Clearly, the best possible thing that could happen to this ungrateful brat and her criminally indulgent father would be for them to be permanently separated from one another. So, Ms. Spanx, I am tempted to grant your request.

BRITLEY. Ha. Eat it, Daddy.

FRANK. I'm so happy for you, princess.

> (**SHANE** *clears his throat loudly.*)

JACKIE. However, it is not the habit of this court to separate a family that is so clearly...what's the word?

SHANE. Loving.

JACKIE. Yes. That is certainly what these two people are. Ruling for the defendant.

BRITLEY. Wait, what?

JACKIE. You've been burned, and we're adjourned.

BRITLEY. Daddy. I didn't get what I want!

    (She storms out.)

FRANK. *(To* **JACKIE**.*)* I hope you're happy.

    (He exits.)

SHANE. That was beautiful, Jackie-lantern. A touching reunion of father and child. The triumph of parental love.

JACKIE. That was the single dirtiest experience of my entire life, and I was married to a Tea Partier.

SHANE. The [**His Name**]* ratings are through the roof. In fact, I see only one way they can possibly go higher.

    (He takes out a contract and hands it to her.)

JACKIE. What's this?

SHANE. It's a contract, permanently changing the name of this show to *Celeb Couple Cases*.

JACKIE. *Celeb Couple Cases*? You think you can turn us into a carbon copy of *Celebrity Couples Court*?

SHANE. Don't be ridiculous. *Celeb Couple Cases* won't be anything like *Celebrity Couples Court.*

JACKIE. If you'll excuse me, I need to purge the last remaining chunks of my soul.

    (She exits.)

HENRY. She'll never go for it.

SHANE. I need her signature.

HENRY. I mean, sure, maybe if someone she trusted suggested it, but she doesn't trust you at all.

SHANE. Say that again.

HENRY. Maybe if someone she trusted suggested it?

    [MUSIC NO. 12: "GET HER TO SIGN"]

---

*Name of rating first established in Act I with male audience member (first appears on page 31 of script).

SHANE. You're a genius, Hank.

HENRY. I am?

SHANE. You are.

> THINK WHAT'LL HAPPEN IF WE GET CANCELLED.
> POOR LITTLE JACKIE, SHE'LL BE DESTROYED.
> THE SHOW IS HER BABY, IT'S ALL SHE'S GOT NOW.
> IT CAN'T BE AVOIDED,
> HER LIFE'S ON THE LINE, HENRY.
> YOU'VE GOT TO SAVE HER, THIS IS YOUR SHOT NOW.
> OH HENRY, GET HER TO SIGN.

HENRY. Me? You want me to –

SHANE. Come now, Henry…

> THINK HOW REWARDING YOU FIND YOUR JOB, SON.
> FEELINGS OF PRIDE YOU CANNOT CURTAIL.
> OH WHAT A BLISSFUL SOURCE OF ENJOYMENT
> JUST BEING HER BAILIFF,
> IT'S SIMPLY DIVINE, HENRY.
> HOW WILL YOU FEEL THEN ON UNEMPLOYMENT?
> OH HENRY, GET HER TO SIGN.

HENRY. I could never betray her.

> *(He starts to exit.)*

SHANE. Have you told her how you feel yet, Hank?

> *(**HENRY** stops.)*

HENRY. What did you say?

SHANE. You think I don't see the way you look at her?

> PICTURE HER, PICTURE YOU,
> YOU'RE THE PERFECT HAPPY TWO.
> PERFECT PICKET FENCE SURROUNDS YOUR PERFECT LAWN.
>
> YOUR THREE KIDS RUN AND PLAY
> AS YOU LAUGH AND SMILE ALL DAY.
> THEN YOU SNUGGLE NEXT TO HER FROM DUSK TO DAWN.
>
> NOW YOU KNOW WHAT TO DO
> SO THESE DREAMS CAN ALL COME TRUE.
> YESSIR, HENRY, THE SHOW MUST GO ON.
> HERE'S WHAT'LL HAPPEN IF WE GET CANCELLED.

YOUR LITTLE CRUSH, WELL, IT'S AT AN END.
SHE'S GONE FOREVER, DON'T YOU MISTAKE IT.
BUT IF WE EXTEND, WELL,
YOUR CHANCES LOOK FINE, HENRY.
THIS IS YOUR SHOT, BOY, GO ON AND TAKE IT.
OH HENRY, GET HER TO SIGN.
OH HENRY, GET HER TO SIGN.
GET HER TO SIGN.
GET HER TO SIGN.

(**SHANE** *exits with the contract.* **HENRY** *debates for a moment, then, defeated follows. Enter* **JACKIE,** *drinking.*)

[MUSIC NO. 12A: "DRUNKEN JACKIE"]

JACKIE. Judge Jackie Justice, host of *Celeb Couple Cases.*

(*She takes a drink.*)

Judge Jackie Justice, host of the number one show on daytime television, *Celeb Couple Cases.*

(*Another drink.*)

Judge Jackie Justice, one-time aspiring Supreme Court Justice, and host of the number one show on television, *Celeb Couple –*

(*Looks at the bottle.*)

I'm gonna need a bigger bottle.

(**JORGE** *appears.*)

[MUSIC NO. 12B: "JORGE, AGAIN!"]

JORGE. *Hola, Señora.*

JACKIE. Jorge?

JORGE. *Sí,* it is me, Jorge de Amor.

JACKIE. I know.

JORGE. I know chu know. Sometimes I just like to say my own name.

JACKIE. If you'll excuse me, Jorge, I have make up a list of celebrity couples who won't make me want to walk into traffic.

JORGE. But, *Señora*, what happen to truth, justice, *y...de amor?*

JACKIE. The fictitious ideals of a fictitious television program.

JORGE. These ideals, *Señora*, chusing the television to pursue them...this is why chu do what chu do. This is everything chu believe in. Just like...

ALL FOUR. JORGE DE AMOR.

(He disappears.)

JACKIE. Maybe. Maybe you're –

(He reappears.)

JORGE. And if there is one thing Jorge de Amor stand for, other than *de amor*, it is that when chu believe in something, chu must fight for that something.

(He disappears.)

JACKIE. You know what? You're absolutely right. If I want my show to stand for truth and justice, to make a difference in real people's lives, then I've got to fight for it.

(Enter **HENRY.***)*

HENRY. Oh. Hello, your Honor.

JACKIE. Take a letter, Henry: Dear Brainless. Never in all my years have I met anyone as nearsighted, blockheaded, or generally stupid as you.

HENRY. Your Honor?

JACKIE. I'm not about to sell out to a bunch of celebrities, I don't care if the show does get cancelled and I never see anyone associated with it ever again, I'm not going to give in to his cockamamie –

HENRY. Maybe you should.

JACKIE. I beg your pardon?

HENRY. I just think that...perhaps...in this particular instance...maybe...you should sign the contract.

(He pulls out the contract.)

JACKIE. This is what you really believe? You think we should change our show to this...this...*Celeb Couple Crap?*

HENRY. Our show?

JACKIE. You've stood by my side since the beginning, Henry.

HENRY. I have, your Honor.

JACKIE. And I've always...I've always...respected you.

HENRY. Yes, your Honor.

JACKIE. I guess that's what makes this so hard...

HENRY. I know, your Honor.

JACKIE. You're fired.

HENRY. What?

JACKIE. You're fired.

HENRY. But...your Honor –

> **[MUSIC NO. 12C: "DON'T NONE OF Y'ALL MOVE, NOW!"]**
>
> (**DUANE** *enters, wearing a trench coat.*)

DUANE. Don't none of y'all move now!

JACKIE. Not this redneck.

DUANE. I mean it. Stay where y'all is, or I'ma blow this courtroom sky high.

> (*He takes off his coat, revealing numerous large fireworks duct taped to his body.*)

HENRY. Jeez Louise!

JACKIE. That has got to be the sorriest excuse for a bomb anybody has ever brought into this courtroom. What kind of backwoods cracker jack box did you find that in?

DUANE. These is fireworks. Ain't none a y'all's mamas never let y'all play with no fireworks when y'all was kids?

> (**HENRY** *draws his gun.*)

HENRY. Don't make any sudden moves.

DUANE. Yessir. Soon as I light this here fuse, this whole courtroom's gonna go up in the biggest, and brightest, and bestest fireworks display [**County Of Production**] ever seen.

HENRY. Put the lighter down.

DUANE. You think you scare me? You think death scare me? Let me tell you somethin', mister, I seen worse'n death. Thanks to this judge lady's 'strainin' order, I seen the blackest, darkest, most soul-achin', glass-chewin' agony any man's ever seen. Yessir, I seen life without Luanne.

HENRY. Your Honor, I think you'd better vacate the courtroom.

JACKIE. I'm not gonna abandon my courtroom just because this lunatic has an unhealthy infatuation with the only woman alive with more dental issues than he has.

HENRY. I don't think your trademark wit is necessarily the best choice in the given situation.

DUANE. Alright, here goes.

HENRY. Wait! Let the judge go.

DUANE. Naw. This judge lady is the whole reason –

HENRY. But, think how impressed Luanne will be by your chivalry, as demonstrated by your decision not to blow up any women or children, excluding audience members.

DUANE. Say, that's pretty good, mister. Alright, the judge lady can go.

JACKIE. Henry –

HENRY. Please, Jackie.

JACKIE. Don't think this means you win, Buster. Someday you'll learn that if you're gonna blow up a courtroom, you'd better have the decency to wear sleeves.

(She exits.)

HENRY. Okay. It's just you and me.

(Re: audience.)

And all of them.

(**JACKIE** *reenters.*)

JACKIE. Henry?

HENRY. Yes?

JACKIE. You called me Jackie. I've never heard you call me Jackie.

HENRY. I'm sorry, your Honor.

JACKIE. No. No, Henry. It was…uh…it was…

HENRY. Just…please. Go.

(*She does.*)

DUANE. Oh. Oh. Oh ho ho, ho ho! Y'all is in love with the judge.

HENRY. What? No.

DUANE. Yes y'all is. I seen it. I seen it right there!

HENRY. So what if I am? Is that such a crime? Is being in love really that insane?

DUANE. Yup.

HENRY. What?

DUANE. Mister, love is the most insanest thing there is. That's why I got me these here fireworks.

HENRY. I don't understand.

DUANE. I even arranged it so's they spell out Luanne's name. L-U- … Anne.

HENRY. You're going to set them off, and you'll be strapped to them at the time?

DUANE. That's how I's winnin' Luanne back.

HENRY. That doesn't make sense.

DUANE. Exactly.

HENRY. What?

DUANE. Let me ask you this, if you is such an expert: What's yer plan?

HENRY. Well… I suppose now that she's fired me there won't be a conflict of interest…so… I don't know, I imagine I could give her a greeting card that adequately expresses my feelings for her.

DUANE. See? That there's a perfectly logical plan.

HENRY. Thank you.

DUANE. That's why it won't never work.

HENRY. What?

[MUSIC NO. 13: "CRAZY AS LOVE"]

DUANE.

> GIRLS IS LIKE TOTALLY BONKERS.
> AND GUYS IS ALL PLUMB OFF THEY BUTTS.
> FOLKS SAYS THAT LOVE ALWAYS CONQUERS.
> BUT I SAYS THAT LOVE CAIN'T CURE NUTS.
>
> PEOPLE, THEY GO PLAIN BANANAS,
> WHEN LOVE IS WHAT THEY'S TRAVELIN' TOWARDS.
> FROM TEXAS TO BOTH THEM MONTANAS,
> LOVE DRIVES US ALL OFF OUR GOURDS.
>
> IF Y'ALL WANT TO SHOW YOU'RE ROMANTIC,
> OR PROVE TO A GIRL SHE'S YOUR DOVE,
> Y'ALL BETTER DO SOMETHING GIGANTIC.
> SOMETHING THAT'S CRAZY,
> CRAZY AS LOVE.
>
> I SEE THAT MY THEORY DON'T SIT WELL.
> Y'ALL THINK THAT MY SCREWS AIN'T TOO TIGHT.
> BUT SOON AS THIS FUSE HERE GETS LIT, WELL,
> Y'ALL GONNA LEARN THAT I'M RIGHT.
>
> THEN LUANNE WILL SEE SHE'S MISTAKEN.
> SHE'LL KNOW THAT WHEN PUSH COME TO SHOVE,
> THESE FIREWORKS PROVE I WEREN'T FAKIN',
> SHE'LL SEE I'M CRAZY,
> CRAZY AS LOVE.
>
> I SEEN THE WORLD WITHOUT LUANNE.
> FER ONCE IT MADE SENSE TO MY BRAIN.
>
> I SEEN THAT THERE LOGICAL, SENSIBLE WORLD,
> BUT HERE'S THE THING I CAIN'T EXPLAIN:
>
> IF THAT'S THE WORLD WITHOUT LUANNE,
> I'D RATHER BE BATSHIT INSANE.

SO, I STUFFED SPARKLERS INTO MY POCKETS.
GOT ALL THEM BLACK CATS I COULD BUY.
AND DUCT TAPED MYSELF TO SOME ROCKETS.
TO WRITE LUANNE'S NAME 'CROSS THE SKY.

OUR LOVE, IT'LL NEVER BURN BRIGHTER.
WITH ALL THEM THERE STARS UP ABOVE.
CUZ SOON AS I LIGHT THIS HERE LIGHTER,
SHE'LL SEE I'M CRAZY,
SHE DROVE ME CRAZY.
LIKE TOTALLY CRAZY.
CRAZY AS –

(Enter **LUANNE**.*)*

LUANNE. Baby?

DUANE. Luanne?

LUANNE. What the hell is you doin'?

DUANE. Nothin'.

LUANNE. Y'all wuz about to blow yerself up? Fer me?

DUANE. Well…

LUANNE. That is the most romantical thing any feller's ever done fer me.

(She pulls him to her, and they kiss.)

Now come on home, and let's get real crazy.

DUANE. Oh, I cain't. I think I'm sorta under arrest again.

HENRY. No, you're not. I don't really have the…

(Re: his gun.)

This is a prop.

DUANE. But we still got that there 'strainin' order.

LUANNE. Nuh-uh, baby. I got it figgered out. Know where 'strainin' orders don't work none?

DUANE. Where?

LUANNE. Space.

DUANE. Y'all didn't.

LUANNE.

> IN OUR SPACESHIP.
> I BUILT A SPACESHIP.
> DON'T NEED NO BUNKER, DUANE, I JIST NEED YOU.
> WE'LL FLY TO SAFETY.
> 'TWEEN MARS AND PLUTO.

DUANE AND LUANNE.

> WE'LL EAT MARSHMALLOW PEEPS IN OUR SPACESHIP BUILT
>   FER TWO.

DUANE. Aw, Luanne. Y'all is jist the best.

LUANNE. Now all I need is a way to launch it.

DUANE. Well, I got a bunch of fireworks.

LUANNE. Then what is we waitin' fer?

> *(They start to exit.)*

DUANE. Oh. Mister?

HENRY. Mm-hm?

DUANE. I don't know how we kin ever repay you.

HENRY. Actually, there may be a way.

LUANNE. What is y'all thinkin'?

HENRY. Well, I thought I'd...

> ### *[MUSIC NO. 13A: "CRAZY AS LOVE REPRISE"]*

> *(**HENRY** whispers to **DUANE**.)*

Then maybe...

> *(More whispering.)*

And finally.

> *(More whispering.)*

DUANE. Now that there is a crazy plan.

> *(They exit.)*

HENRY.

> LOVE IS A CRAZY EMOTION.
> IT CAN'T BE ENCASED IN A CARD.
> WITH LOVE THAT'S AS BIG AS THE OCEAN,
> EXPRESSING IT CAN BE, WELL, HARD.

LOVE IS ABOUT TAKING CHANCES.
LIKE THIS PLAN THAT I'M THINKING OF.
I'LL SHOW JACKIE WHAT TRUE ROMANCE IS.
I'LL DO SOMETHING CRAZY,
CAUSE SHE DRIVES ME CRAZY.
LIKE PLUMB BATSHIT CRAZY.
CRAZY AS LOVE.

(Enter **JACKIE**.)

JACKIE. Henry?

HENRY. Yes, your Honor?

JACKIE. You risked your life. For me.

HENRY. Well, I don't know if I'd say –

JACKIE. I'm sorry, Henry. I should never have fired you. You'll always have a job here at *Celeb Couple Cases*.

HENRY. Wait, you mean –

JACKIE. Give me the contract.

HENRY. Your Honor –

JACKIE. I'll sign it, Henry. If it's what you think we should do, I'll give my consent to change the show into whatever he wants. Just, promise you'll find somebody adequate to replace me.

HENRY. What are you saying?

JACKIE. I'd like you to give Shane my resignation. Now, if you'll kindly get out of my way, I need to purchase a small tropical island on which I can live out the remainder of my days in euphoric seclusion.

HENRY. No.

JACKIE. I'm sorry, what did you say?

HENRY. I said no, your Honor.

[MUSIC NO. 13B: "JUDGE JACKIE REPRISE #4"]

JACKIE. You've never said no to me in your life.

HENRY. There's still one case left on the docket.

JACKIE. I'll be damned if I'm going to preside over another one of Shane's farcical lunacies.

HENRY. You won't be presiding over anything.

JACKIE. You're not making any sense.

HENRY. All rise. This court is now in session.

JACKIE. What do you think you're doing?

HENRY. This is the plaintiff, Henry Winslow. He claims that the defendant has allowed the pain she's suffered to suffocate her true romantic nature.

JACKIE. Henry –

HENRY. This is the defendant, Jackie Justinowitz, A.K.A. the Honorable Judge Jackie Justice. She stands charged with the murder of love. We now call to order the Case of the Jaded Judge.

> NOW I'LL SHOW YOU HER INFRACTIONS,
> AND THE EVIDENCE THEREOF.
> YES, THIS CASE HERE IS BOUND TO BE A THRILLER.
> WATCH ME AS I GRILL HER,
> AND PROVE THAT SHE'S THE KILLER OF LOVE.

HENRY & ALL.

> JUDGE JACKIE JUSTICE.
> JUDGE JACKIE JUSTICE.
> JUDGE JACKIE JUSTICE.

JACKIE. This is preposterous. Who is supposed to render a verdict?

HENRY. They will.

JACKIE. Who?

HENRY. Them. The people. You will be judged by a jury of your peers, your Honor.

JACKIE. My peers? Henry, some of them look like they're from [**Lower Class Neighborhood**].

HENRY. Zip it, your Honor. You're not in charge anymore. How do you plead?

JACKIE. Not guilty.

HENRY. The people call Duane Duaneson and Luanne Pumpkinblotch.

*(Enter **DUANE** and **LUANNE**.)*

[MUSIC NO. 13C: "CASE MONTAGE"]

JACKIE. I issued a restraining order against these two yokels.

HENRY. Mr. Duaneson, are you aware that you are violating the terms of a direct court order?

DUANE. Yup.

HENRY. And why are you willing to do so?

LUANNE. We'ze in love.

JACKIE. This is ridiculous.

HENRY. The people call Treat Macklin and Poo-Bear Daniels.

>*(The actors quickly change into* **TREAT** *and* **POO-BEAR**.*)*

JACKIE. Henry –

HENRY. Ms. Daniels, why did you ask Mr. Macklin to get your name tattooed on his chest?

POO-BEAR. I already say, he my boo.

HENRY. And Mr. Macklin, even for just half of the tattoo, was the process painful?

TREAT. Oh, mos def. It be all boom!

JACKIE. Another example of the destructive –

HENRY. The people call Frank and Britley Spanx.

JACKIE. This is completely insane.

>*(They change into* **FRANK** *and* **BRITLEY**.*)*

HENRY. Mr. Spanx, your daughter is an obnoxious, ungrateful, spoiled pain in the neck, yet, you opposed her attempt at emancipation. Why?

FRANK. She's my daughter. I love her.

BRITLEY. OMG, Daddy. Just, like, kill me. Kill me.

HENRY. All of these people know that love might hurt them. And yet…

JACKIE. They're morons.

HENRY. Choosing pain is proof of being a moron?

JACKIE. Yes.

HENRY. Then I have one final set of witnesses to call.

MAN 1. Seriously?

HENRY. The people call Brooks Billingston and Marjorie Merryweather.

WOMAN 1. I don't even remember who that is.

HENRY. The pizza people.

WOMAN 1. Right.

(They change into BROOKS and MARJORIE.)

JACKIE. What are you getting at here?

HENRY. Ms. Merryweather, will you hand Mr. Billingston this slice of pizza?

MARJORIE. If you say so.

(She does.)

HENRY. Do not eat that pizza, Mr. Billingston. The cheese is scalding hot.

BROOKS. Yeah, okay.

(He looks at the pizza. Beat. Again. Beat. He takes a huge bite.)

Oh Jethuth!

JACKIE. You see? You see how stupid these nutjobs are?

HENRY. Mr. Billingston, why did you choose to eat that piping hot pizza?

BROOKS. Becauthe, it'th tho delithiouth.

HENRY. He eats the pizza because it's delicious.

JACKIE. He's a moron.

HENRY. Have you ever been in love, your Honor?

(Enter YOUNG ALLISTER.)

YOUNG ALLISTER. Hello there, Jackie.

JACKIE. Of course not.

YOUNG ALLISTER. May I have this dance?

HENRY. Might I remind you that you are under oath?

JACKIE. Alright. Yes. I was in love. Once. But that was a long time ago.

[MUSIC NO. 14: "NOT ME REPRISE"]

HENRY. And what happened?

 (No response.)

 Your Honor? What happened?

JACKIE.

 YEARS AGO I LET LOVE WIN.
 OPENED UP, LET SOMEONE IN.
 AND IT WAS, WELL, UTTERLY FULFILLING.

 ALL TOO SOON, HE BROKE MY HEART.
 LIKE A FOOL I FELL APART.
 ALL THESE YEARS, I'VE BLAMED HIM FOR LOVE'S KILLING.

 BUT IT WAS ME.
 IT WAS ME.
 NOW AT LAST I CAN SEE.
 I'VE STAYED DISTANT AND COLD TO ENSURE LOVE COULD
  NEVER TAKE HOLD.

 LOOK AT ME.
 LOOK AT ME.
 FREE FROM LOVE'S TYRANNY.
 I HAVE SWORN TO STAY NUMB, SO THAT'S WHAT I'VE
  BECOME.
 ALL ALONE AS I'VE CHOSEN TO BE.
 IT WAS ME.

I had my heart broken, Henry. And ever since, I've made the decision to cut myself off from the possibility of ever being hurt like that again. I killed love, Henry.

HENRY. Well then your Honor, to paraphrase a wise woman, you are a moron.

[MUSIC NO. 15: "PIZZA IS DELICIOUS"]

JACKIE. What are you talking about?

HENRY.

 PIZZA IS DELICIOUS,
 THOUGH IT'S OFTEN PAINFUL TOO.
 IT BURNS US SOMETHING VICIOUS,
 STILL, WE CHEW.

HENRY.

> LOVE CAN LEAVE US BAWLING.
> WHEN IT'S SNUFFED OUT LIKE A FLAME.
> STILL WE KEEP ON FALLING
> ALL THE SAME.
>
> YES, YOUR PAST HAS BEEN UNFAIR,
> BUT DON'T LET THAT MASK THE JOY.
> THERE'S PLEASURE THAT THE PAIN CANNOT DESTROY.
>
> SO, I'M DOWN HERE ON MY KNEES.
> AND I'M BEGGING JACKIE, PLEASE.
> WON'T YOU LET SOMEBODY BE YOUR PIZZA CHEESE?
>
> WOULD IT CHANGE YOUR MIND IF YOU ONLY KNEW?
> JACKIE JUSTICE, I'M IN LOVE WITH YOU.

JACKIE. Henry, I...I...I had no idea.

HENRY. Unfortunately, the charges still stand. And your confession has been entered into evidence.

JACKIE. But –

HENRY. I will, however, instruct the jury to consider a plea of not guilty by reason of temporary insanity.

JACKIE. You want me to say I was crazy?

HENRY. If I've learned anything, it's that love is a state of insanity. So, ladies and gentlemen of the jury, it is now your turn to Judge Jackie Justice. If you find her not guilty by reason of temporary insanity, please do so by show of applause.

[MUSIC NO. 15A: "VOTING"]

(Hopefully, they do.)

Well, your Honor, it seems that the people have been swayed by your argument and have found you not guilty.

JACKIE. I...I'm overwhelmed.

HENRY. Unfortunately, even temporary insanity carries with it a rather severe sentence.

JACKIE. And what's that?

HENRY. That is up to the people to decide. There are three possible sentences, your Honor. The first is dinner.

With a certain charming bailiff. The second possible sentence is breakdancing.

JACKIE. I'm sorry, did you say…

HENRY. Breakdancing, your Honor. To a distinctly '80s beat.

JACKIE. Oh dear lord.

HENRY. The final possible sentence would require you to [Play The Accordion]*.

JACKIE. The [Accordion]?

HENRY. It's out of my hands. Your fate rests with the people now. Ladies and gentlemen of the jury, if you think that she should be sentenced to dinner with her boyishly handsome sidekick, please applaud now. [Option #1]

> *(Pause for applause.)*

If you would like to see the judge breakdance, applaud now. [Option # 2]

> *(Pause for applause.)*

And finally, if you would like to hear Judge Jackie attempt to [Play The Accordion], please applaud now. [Option #3]

> *(Pause for applause.)*

OPTION #1

HENRY. Well, your Honor, it seems that the people think your most suitable punishment would be dinner with me.

[MUSIC NO. 16: "THE TRIALS OF LOVE"]

JACKIE. Henry, you are the kindest, most considerate, most understanding person I have ever met. When I think that, after all these years of shutting love out, I might

---

*Talent can be replaced with bizarre, unexpected skill of the actor in question.

be lucky enough to open myself up to someone like you, I…I don't know what to say.

HENRY. I believe the people have spoken.

(Skip to song.)

OPTION #2 OR OPTION #3

HENRY. Well, that didn't go exactly as I had hoped.

JACKIE. Never let it be said that I'm a woman to commune a sentence.

(She breakdances or performs random talent.)

HENRY. You are surprisingly good at that.

JACKIE. Henry, does this rule out sentence one as a possibility?

HENRY. Your Honor?

JACKIE. Dinner? Is that off the table?

HENRY. You still want to go to dinner with me?

[MUSIC NO. 16: "THE TRIALS OF LOVE"]

JACKIE. Henry, you are the kindest, most considerate, most understanding person I have ever met. When I think that, after all these years of shutting love out, I might be lucky enough to open myself up to someone like you, I… I don't know what to say.

HENRY. I believe the people have spoken.

(End of Options #2 and #3.)

LOVERS ARE BLIND.
THAT'S WHAT THEY SAY.
BUMBLING THROUGH NIGHT IN SEARCH OF THE DAWN.

BUT TAKE MY HAND,
WE'LL FIND A WAY.
FUMBLING BUT STUMBLING ON.

THROUGH THE TRIALS OF LOVE.
THE TRIALS OF LOVE.

THROUGH THE TRIALS OF LOVE.
THE TRIALS OF LOVE.

(Enter **SHANE.***)*

SHANE. The [**His Name**]* ratings are off the charts, Jackie-cakes. Why, the love story between the two of you should carry us through the next five seasons. I've taken the liberty of drawing up a new contract –

JACKIE. You know what? I've had just about enough of network television. Henry, get me the number for the people at Netflix.

SHANE. Netflix? No, not Netflix. Anything but Netflix. We've got sponsors lining up –

JACKIE. Shane? Blow it out your ass.

LOVE IS A LEAP.
THE DANGER IS REAL.
TRYING TO FLY IS RISKING THE FALL.

BOTH.

BUT IF WE DON'T
WE'LL NEVER FEEL
THE FEELING OF FLYING AT ALL.

OH THE TRIALS OF LOVE.
THE TRIALS OF LOVE.
OH THE TRIALS OF LOVE.
THE TRIALS OF LOVE.

OH THE TRIALS OF LOVE.
THE TRIALS OF LOVE.
FACING THE TRIALS OF LOVE.

(Enter **DUANE** *and* **LUANNE.***)*

LUANNE. Duane Duaneson, y'all has got to be the biggest ijit in ten counties. I cain't even describe how much I hate y'all.

---

*Name of rating first established in Act I with male audience member (first appears on page 31 of script).

JACKIE. I'm sorry, did you just say you hate the man with whom you are about to spend the rest of your life trapped inside a tiny, homemade spaceship?

DUANE. Yes'm.

LUANNE. I hate him more'n life itself. That's how's I know I love him so much.

SOMETIMES IN LOVE

Y'ALL HATE HIS GUTS.

WAIT 'TIL YA SEE THE DUMB THINGS HE DOES.

DUANE & LUANNE.

BUT EVEN THOUGH

SHE'LL DRIVE YA NUTS,

YA LOVE EVEN MORE JIST BECUZ.

ALL.

OH THE TRIALS OF LOVE.

OH THE TRIALS OF LOVE.

OH THE TRIALS OF LOVE.

OH THE TRIALS OF LOVE.

OH THE TRIALS OF LOVE.

OH THE TRIALS OF LOVE.

FACING THE TRIALS OF LOVE.

LUANNE.

IT AIN'T ROSES OR MORNIN' GLORIES.

DUANE.

IT'S MORE LIKE A THORN OR A WEED.

LUANNE.

IT AIN'T ONE OF THEM FANCY STORIES

DUANE.

FER FANCY FOLKS WHO KIN READ.

JACKIE.

YOU MAY FIND THE CONCEPT DISDAINFUL.

HENRY.

IT MAY BE A THOUGHT YOU REVILE.

JACKIE.

BUT THOUGH IT CAN OFTEN BE PAINFUL,

ALL.

LOVE IS WHAT MAKES LIFE WORTHWHILE.

SHANE. Well, all's well that ends well. For me, at least. I'm happy to report that the government is forming a new commission to regulate adorable videos of cats, babies, and people lighting farts on fire. And guess who they've tapped to head it up. Yessir, you're looking at an official Agent of the Federal –

> *(He holds out a badge.)*

LUANNE. Great Xantos on High, Duane. It's the guv'ment.

SHANE. I beg your pardon.

DUANE. Luanne, what you think happens to guv'ments when y'all launch 'em from space?

SHANE. Come again?

LUANNE. I reckon we'ze 'bout to find out.

SHANE. Oh dear.

> *(They chase him off.)*

JACKIE. This isn't going to be easy for me, Henry.

HENRY. For me either, your Honor.

JACKIE. I wish it were like in the movies. Where there's a big climactic sign to tell us we've made the right decision.

HENRY. What, some definitive symbol of the explosive power of love and the bright, booming triumph of the human spirit?

JACKIE. Seems pretty ridiculous, doesn't it?

LUANNE. *(Off stage.)* Light that there lighter, Duane!

> *(The sound of a fuse being lit, followed by a hiss as the craft blasts off, then the explosion of numerous fireworks.)*

HENRY. Fireworks.

JACKIE. Well, what do you know?

> *(We see DUANE and LUANNE, flying in their spaceship, dragging SHANE along behind.)*

HENRY AND JACKIE.
LOVE IS A FLAME.
LOVE IS A FIRE.
LOVE LEAVES A BRIGHT INDELIBLE MARK.

HENRY AND JACKIE. *(cont.)*
> THOUGH IT MAY BURN,
> STILL IT CLIMBS HIGHER.
> LOVE LIGHTS THE NIGHT LIKE A SPARK.

ALL.
> OH THE TRIALS OF LOVE.
> OH THE TRIALS OF LOVE.
> OH THE TRIALS OF LOVE.
> OH THE TRIALS OF LOVE.
>
> OH THE TRIALS OF LOVE.
> OH THE TRIALS OF LOVE.
> MAKING OUR WAY THROUGH THE TRIALS OF LOVE.
>
> THROUGH THE TRIALS OF LOVE.
> THROUGH THE TRIALS OF LOVE.
> THROUGH THE TRIALS OF LOVE.
> JUDGE JACKIE JUSTICE.

>   (**JACKIE** *grabs* **HENRY** *and kisses him.*)

> JUDGE JACKIE JUSTICE.

End of Play